EXTREME MEASURES

A NOVEL OF SUSPENSE

EXTREME MEASURES

BY BESTSELLING AUTHOR

MICHELE ASHMAN BELL

Covenant Communications, Inc.

Covenant

Cover image Line of Trees © Sebastian Knight, courtesy iStockphoto.com.

Cover design copyright © 2015 by Covenant Communications, Inc.

Published by Covenant Communications, Inc.
American Fork, Utah

Printed in the United States of America
First Printing: May 2015

21 20 19 18 17 16 15   10 9 8 7 6 5 4 3 2 1

ISBN 978-1-68047-165-6

This book is dedicated to the amazing men in my life:

To my father, Nolan Earl Ashman.
You've shown me the true meaning of love and selfless service.

To my husband, Gary.
Thank you for your love and support and for being an incredible husband, father, and grandfather.

To my son, Weston, my hero.
Your strength, your example of faith, and your ability to laugh when sometimes things just aren't funny has lifted me when I didn't think I could even stand.

To my son-in-law Brandon.
You are such a blessing to our family, and I'm so glad you and Kendyl found each other. I'm grateful for your big heart and contagious laugh.

To my son-in-law Austin.
No one is more perfect for Andi than you are. I never get tired of your energy, enthusiasm, and your fabulous way of telling stories. You inspire me.

1

EMMA LOWELL PULLED THE VIBRATING cell phone from her coat pocket and looked at the name of the caller . . . and groaned.

It was Margaret.

Emma's former mother-in-law called every day, sometimes twice. And now that Emma was engaged and getting married soon, she called even more often.

It wasn't that Emma didn't care about Margaret, but the woman couldn't seem to accept and understand that Emma was moving on with her life. Emma had tried. Truly, she had. For two years she had tried to make marriage with Jonathan work. But discovery of repeated infidelities had led to a confrontation, in which he had told her to accept that a man having extramarital affairs was "only human." They had been separated for almost a year when Emma received news Jonathan had died.

She stuffed the phone back into her pocket. She would call Margaret back tomorrow. Tonight was about her and Landon.

"Anything important?" Landon asked, pulling his new BMW X5 SUV into the restaurant parking lot. A spot was open near the entrance.

"Nothing that can't wait till tomorrow."

As he got out of the car and walked around to her side, she glanced down at the sparkling princess-cut diamond engagement ring on her finger and smiled. She didn't have to pinch herself anymore. The ring was a wonderful reminder that it was really happening. She was getting married.

Landon reached for her hand and helped her out of the car. They embraced and kissed briefly.

"Have I told you how much I love you?" he said.

"Not since we left my house."

"Well then, I love you Emma Lowell soon-to-be Reed."

"And I love you, Landon I-can't-wait-to-be-your-wife Reed."

They both knew they were cheesy and ridiculously in love, but they didn't care. She had never been so happy in her life.

Holding hands they walked toward the restaurant. The sunset over Puget Sound bathed the shoreline with golden orange rays.

Landon had surprised her on New Year's Eve and proposed to her, giving her a ring she never would have dared to hope for. The moment had been magical, like a fairytale. She was marrying Landon, the man of her dreams, and not only that, she loved his family and they loved her. It was ideal. As much as she'd loved Jonathan, her marriage to him, and her relationship with his family, had been anything but ideal.

She'd grown and changed since Jonathan's death. Not only had she changed careers, leaving behind the pressure and stress of her job at the advertising firm where she'd worked as a graphic designer, she had started her own photography business. Her calendar was scheduled months out for weddings and family photos. She loved her job.

She'd also made a complete one hundred and eighty-degree turn in her life spiritually.

When she'd turned eight, she'd been baptized into The Church of Jesus Christ of Latter-day Saints, but neither of her parents had been active, so consequently she never went to church, except when her grandmother took her. Even though she didn't go very often, she loved going to church and learning about Jesus. In fact, the teachings she remembered as a young girl helped her greatly when Jonathan died, enough so that she looked up the LDS missionaries and asked them to teach her the lessons. That was how she met Landon. He'd been serving as the ward mission leader in her area and had helped teach her and support her as she began going to church and became active again. Her testimony for the gospel grew quickly, and so did her love for Landon. Things about life that confused her before finally began to make sense. The whole purpose of life and what happened after death were teachings that soothed her soul. That had been seven months ago. And now, in a few more months, she would realize her dream of being sealed for eternity to Landon. They would find a home that needed work and fix it up together, raise a family, and grow old together. He was the love of her life, her best friend and sweetheart. After all the hell she'd been through the last few years, she was finally getting her happy ending.

"Emma," Landon's voice interrupted her thoughts, "we're being seated."

Jarred back to her reality, she looked at her hunky Prince Charming as he led her to their table. The waitress handed them each a menu and promised to be right back with the ice water they requested.

Emma looked across the table at Landon and wished they didn't have to wait six months to get sealed. But, in order for Landon's parents to be home from Brazil, where his dad was serving as mission president, they needed to wait.

She'd never met them personally, but with the help of video chatting, she and Landon had spent a good deal of time talking to his mom and occasionally his dad while they were out of the country. Even across the miles she felt a connection to them, and they had expressed the same. She couldn't wait to meet them in person.

"Are we ready to order?" the waitress asked after giving them several minutes to decide.

Emma glanced one last time at the menu in front of her. "I'll have the spinach salad with the dressing on the side, and could you add the grilled chicken breast too, please?"

"Certainly, ma'am." The waitress added Landon's order of filet mignon and garlic potatoes and promised to be right back. Emma didn't care how long she took. She was content to sit at the table with Landon for hours and look out the picture windows that overlooked the ocean. The January evening was unseasonably warm, and the evening sky was completely clear. It was one of those perfect moments that could go on forever as far as she was concerned.

Landon reached for her hand, lifted it to his lips, and kissed her knuckles several times. "Is everything okay? You seem to be lost in thought tonight. Have you got something on your mind?"

Wishing they were sitting side by side in a booth, rather than across from each other at the table, she leaned toward him to get closer.

She loved the natural wave of his hair and the way it fell onto his forehead and curled at the base of his neck. His strong jaw-line and thick brows gave him an air of brooding and sophistication, straight from a Jane Austen novel. But it was his blue eyes that captivated her and held her breathless at times.

"I'm just enjoying this moment with you," she answered. "I know how busy you are getting everything ready before you leave. It means a lot that you would bring me here."

"I always have time for you," he said. "Except for packing, I've got everything done at the office. Some of it I can do on the plane."

"I'm a good packer, if you need my help."

"I'd be tempted to put you in my suitcase so I could take you with me," he teased.

Stuffing her into a suitcase was the only way he'd get her on a plane. Her father, an MD/JD, was a noted malpractice attorney in Seattle who flew his own Cessna Skyhawk plane since most of his clients were out-of-state. Her parents and another couple had flown to Montana for a business meeting then were flying on to Banff, Canada, for a week-long vacation when they got caught in a bizarre downdraft that crashed them into the side of a mountain. Both couples were killed instantly. She knew it was an irrational fear, she'd read and been told the safety statistics of air travel countless times, but the thought of getting into a plane—or of a loved one getting inside a plane—literally made her sick to her stomach. "Did you find out yet if you'll be staying that extra week in Dubai?"

He shook his head and covered their clasped hands with his other hand. "I won't know until we get there. Believe me, after three weeks, I'll be more than ready to come home. I hope we don't have to stay longer. Which reminds me. I found a new phone app that will help you know where I am if for some reason you can't contact me."

"Really?"

"Hand me your phone and I'll set it up for you. It will just take a sec." He was part of a global commercial team for Puget Oil Refinery. His job took him all over the world. Landon had given her a state-of-the-art phone so they could stay in touch no matter where he was. She was surprised at how easy it had been to learn how to use it.

Even with the ability to stay in touch with him, she still struggled with the thought of him leaving for almost a month. Especially in January, the anniversary of her parents' death. It wasn't just that she would miss him—no matter how often he went out of town, she missed him terribly—but that he was flying. It didn't help that he was going to the Middle East, which made it even more difficult. She couldn't bear the thought of losing him. Not now that they'd found each other. Not after all she'd been through and all the loved ones she'd lost.

The gospel had helped her understand and grasp the fact that it was all part of a plan and it was her parents' time to go. As much as she missed them, this knowledge helped her deal with the loss. Especially since she was also dealing with Jonathan's death.

Even though they'd been headed for divorce, she was still heartbroken when she heard he was gone. The circumstances surrounding his death still puzzled her. He'd been found in a strange hotel room, drowned in the bathtub, without his cell phone or any identification. The mystery was never solved, and even though there was no proof, the detective on the case had all but agreed with her that Jonathan had been involved with another woman. Even though there was no sign of foul play, his wallet and money were missing. The media frenzy that followed brought an enormous amount of shame to the family. Emma had distanced herself enough that she was never a target of their interest, but the media dragged the Lowell name through the dirt. Strangely enough, after several months, the case had been dropped and the furor died out. She'd always wondered if somehow Margaret managed to make it go away.

The case had never been solved, but Emma had long suspected Jonathan had had other women in his life, and he'd all but admitted it when she finally confronted him one day. He not only told her that it was common for men to have other women on the side but was completely unapologetic about it. He honestly expected her to accept it and be grateful she was part of the Lowell family.

Jonathan was the son of Charles and Margaret Lowell, of the prominent Boston, Massachusetts, Lowells. The family name had followed them to the Seattle area when Charles became the chief surgeon at Harbor View Hospital, Seattle's best hospital. The Lowells quickly became an integral part of the social structure of the city. Charles had sat on the board of many of the main businesses in the Seattle area, and Margaret was involved in charities and the arts. She had also worked as a nurse for several renowned fertility specialists and was elected to the National Council of State Boards of Nursing. Her professional achievements were impressive, and between her and her late husband, the Lowell family name was respected and carried great power.

At first, Emma hadn't realized the extent of obligation that came with having such an affluent name. Once she fully realized the prestige and expectation though, she began to feel the weight of it. Not only was she expected to attend various functions and events, but she was also to handle herself in the proper manner befitting a wealthy socialite. It was also part of the reason her mother-in-law never deemed her worthy of her son.

She often wondered why the Lowells had left Boston. From the few things Jonathan said about it she came up with her own theory; Charles had too many ex-mistresses there and the best way to avoid any scandal was to not feed the flames of gossip columnists searching for a story.

After she and Jonathan were married, Emma discovered the apple hadn't fallen far from the tree. She'd stayed with Jonathan, trying to ignore gossip and her own suspicions, but his unexplained absences, secret phone calls, and disinterest in her confirmed that he'd been having affairs their whole marriage. When she received the phone call that he'd been found dead in a hotel bathtub, she wasn't even shocked. The autopsy showed the alcohol level in his blood was so high that it was possible he fell asleep in the tub and drowned. There was no proof that someone was with him, but it made sense. She doubted they would ever know the real story, and it really didn't matter to her anymore. She'd gotten closure and had forgiven him for anything he'd done. Becoming hard and embittered by it didn't make sense. She'd given everything she could to her marriage, and that knowledge gave her peace.

Bless Landon's heart for being understanding of her issues and fears. He never pried about Jonathan and always had a listening ear. And he never pressured her about flying, which could have been a problem for them because his job at Puget Oil required that he travel at least two weeks a month, and after they were married she would be able to go with him anywhere he went in the world. Puget Oil had business operations all over Europe, Asia, and the Middle East, but unless it was possible to get there by land or sea, she wouldn't be going with him.

"So, what are you going to do while I'm gone?"

"Well, besides miss you like crazy, I plan on spending weekends house-hunting. Cassie called this afternoon and said there are a couple of places she wants to show me that have everything we're looking for."

"Honey, that's great. She's really determined to help us find a home."

"She's working hard," Emma said. "It's great because I enjoy spending time with her too. She's more a friend than my Realtor. Also, Jess and I have plans to watch some chick-flick movie marathons together and go shopping and out to dinner."

"I get the feeling you're not going to miss me," he said, looking wounded.

"Well, you are wrong about that. The more I stay busy, the faster the time will go. I'm just lucky Jess and Cassie are willing to help keep me entertained. In fact, I've been thinking the two of them should meet. They're two of my favorite people."

"I'll have to think of a way to thank them for taking such good care of you while I'm gone."

Jess and Emma got to be good friends when they were assigned to be visiting teaching companions. They immediately hit it off and had been close ever since. Jess was going to be Emma's maid-of-honor. This was a responsibility Emma knew Jess wouldn't take lightly. If anyone knew how to take care of things and people, and who was loyal to a fault, it was Jess.

"Grab some chocolate while you're in Switzerland," she suggested. "I know they'd like that."

He nodded. "Good idea. I'll do that." He checked something on her phone and handed it to her. "Remind me to show you how to use it before I leave."

"Here we go," the waitress interrupted, setting their plates in front of them.

Emma noticed right off that the chicken on her salad wasn't grilled but breaded and fried. Not one to ever make a scene or draw attention to herself, she said nothing when the waitress asked if there was anything else they needed.

Landon didn't waste any time launching into his food, but after a few bites noticed that Emma was picking the chicken off her salad. She wasn't a fan of deep-fried foods and would rather not eat it.

"Is something wrong?" He looked closer at her meal. "Oh, you ordered grilled chicken. Let's send it back."

"No," she stopped him before he could raise his arm to get the waitress's attention. "It's okay. I'm not that hungry."

"But—"

"It's okay, Landon. Really." She didn't want to cause a scene in front of the other customers in the restaurant or embarrass the waitress.

"Honey, it's not a problem."

"I'm fine. Really," she assured him.

He sighed. "All right then. But I worry that you're too nice."

"Is that possible? Nice is a good thing."

"It is. But people take advantage of you. I don't like that."

"I'll do better. I promise. I'll work on it while you're gone. When you get back I'll be"—she searched for the right word—"feisty."

"Ooh, I like that." He laughed. "If that's the case, I'll let you negotiate the price when we find a home."

Lost in talk about finding their dream home and how much they looked forward to fixing it up together, they forgot about everything around them as they planned their future together.

* * *

Out of habit, Emma checked her phone again as they walked out of the restaurant. She didn't mean to groan; it just sort of slipped out.

"Is there a problem?" Landon slipped his arm around her as they walked through the brisk night air to his car.

"Margaret called. Again." She was never up for a conversation with Jonathan's mother. The woman intimidated, infuriated, and completely exasperated her. It wasn't enough that she'd never let Emma forget she wasn't good enough for her son, but after his death the woman seemed to have this need to have daily contact with Emma. They didn't have enough in common to talk every day, or even once a week. It took too much energy to have a conversation with her.

"Did she leave a message?" Landon unlocked the car and opened the door for Emma.

"I'm sure she did. I'll call her tomorrow. I'm sure it's not urgent."

"Maybe you should listen to her message. Last time you didn't answer, she was calling from the hospital to tell you she'd had a stroke."

Emma collapsed into the seat and closed her eyes, trying to find the strength to face whatever was on the message. She didn't know how to explain it, but sometimes she felt like even though Margaret never approved of her as a daughter-in-law, she expected Emma's devotion and attention daily, even if she had to manipulate it out of Emma. A few months earlier, Margaret had been upset when Emma told her she and Landon were driving to San Francisco for a long weekend, which happened to be the same weekend as Margaret's seventieth birthday. The day after they arrived in San Francisco, Margaret called to tell her she'd had a stroke and desperately needed Emma with her.

Landon tried to be patient when it came to Margaret. He understood that, as a widow whose only son was deceased, she was old and lonely. But he got frustrated when they had to cut their trip short and return to Seattle. Emma still wasn't convinced the woman had suffered a stroke. She never got to talk to the doctor about it, and the nurses couldn't give her the information, so she had no choice but to believe it had happened. From that point on, Margaret used a wheelchair and moved into a care center. But Margaret cried wolf so often that Emma never knew if she was being honest or manipulative.

"I don't want to ruin our evening," Emma said. "I'm willing to take a chance she's okay." She turned her phone off and buried it deep in her purse. Landon was leaving, and she wanted to spend every moment with him that she could.

"Did I tell you we might go skiing when we're in Switzerland?"

"That would be amazing!" She wondered if the fake enthusiasm in her voice was obvious. It was going to be torture having him gone so long.

"John's the one planning this trip, and he's trying to pack in as much as he can. We've got meetings in Cressier, Switzerland, with a company called Petroplus, and while we're there John's determined to go skiing."

"It makes sense," she said, trying to show support, but in her heart she knew she needed to prepare for him to stay that extra week on his "business" trip.

"I guess. I don't have much of a say in any of it. I am excited to go to Cairo. I've always wanted to see the pyramids." He slowed the car as he prepared to stop at a light. "I would love to take you with me to these places someday."

Emma looked away. "I know. Jess told me she has the name of a good therapist; I just need to call and set up an appointment."

"I'm not trying to pressure you. It has to happen when you're ready. I just don't want to be going away on trips and leaving you behind all the time."

"When we have children, I'll have to stay behind anyway."

Not the type to press an issue, Landon let it drop, but Emma knew he was putting up with a lot from her, and she didn't like requiring that of him. Between Margaret and her own personal issues and phobias, she worried he would realize she was just too high maintenance for him. When she voiced her concerns about this, he always told her she was worth the work, but she didn't want to risk damaging their relationship. Her fear of flying translated into fear of riding in any sort of vehicle that could potentially crash. She was fine around town, but getting on the freeway turned her into a nervous wreck. At least when someone else was driving she could find ways to distract herself.

With the setting sun, the temperature had dropped, and the welcome warmth from the seat warmer permeated her coat. She slid deeper into her seat. "Your seat heats up so much faster than the one in my car. I love it."

"You're welcome to drive my car while I'm gone. You might need the 4-wheel drive. I understand there's a possibility of snow this week."

"What? Please tell me you're joking. We are having such beautiful weather."

"Sorry. I heard it on the radio. This is the warm before the storm. An Arctic cold front is coming this way. It could get ugly."

"I don't want to wreck your BMW."

"Sweetie, my SUV will be safer than your Lexus if it does snow. I insist."

"If it snows, I won't be going outside. I have plenty of work I can do from home." Her small photography studio in the corner of her apartment allowed clients to come to her for indoor photo shoots. Landon had promised her an entire room for her studio in their new house. She hoped it would be on a second floor, with a view of Puget Sound.

"I want you to keep it. I'll feel better knowing you have four-wheel drive. Besides, you're driving me to the airport, so you will have it anyway."

She knew when it came to her safety he wouldn't back dow agreed. Dreading the thought of snow and going out in it, e driving in it, made her wonder if she should go to the store and stock up on food and bottled water, just in case.

"What time do you leave again?" she asked, already knowing it was sometime late morning but wishing his answer would surprise her and be a week later.

"We're catching the ten fifteen to Denver. We couldn't get a direct flight, so we land but don't change planes. Then we fly to JFK and have a layover for a few hours before we leave for London. I'll call you."

"Okay," she said quickly as a rush of emotion caught her off guard. She fought to keep her imagination from running away from her. Nothing was going to happen to him. He was going to be okay. He would come home to her.

"Hey," he reached for her hand. "Are you okay?"

She bit her top lip and steadied her emotions with a calming breath. She wasn't okay. Her fear of losing him was almost more than she could bear. She knew she was being ridiculous, but painful memories crowded her heart and brain and left no room for good sense.

Nodding her answer, she gave him an unconvincingly brave smile and knew she just had to go on faith and prayer. Surely God wouldn't take him from her. Not when she'd already lost every loved one close to her.

Landon pulled into the parking stall in front of her apartment and put the car in park but left the engine running. "Thanks for dinner."

"You're welcome. I'm glad it worked out."

They sat in silence. She didn't want their night to end, but it was getting late and he had a big day tomorrow.

"Hey," he reached for her hand, "we'll talk every night. I'll be back before you know it."

She nodded, afraid to speak and release the flood of emotions building up inside of her.

He opened his door and came around to her side of the car. They held hands as they made their way up the walk to her front porch. It was too cold to linger and too late for him to come inside.

"Good night, sweetie. Happy dreams."

"You too," she said, smiling at his often-used parting.

He kissed her briefly and gave her one last hug. Taking her key, he opened the door for her and let her inside. "I'll see you tomorrow."

He pulled the door closed behind him, and his footsteps faded into the night. Emma held it together until he was gone, then she fell onto the couch and cried.

2

EMMA SLEPT IN AND LOUNGED in bed for a while before finally forcing herself to get up. She dreaded taking Landon to the airport today. The thought of him being gone was hard but something she could deal with; the thought of losing him created a feeling of panic inside her chest. She had to force herself to breathe deeply and think of other things so she wouldn't have a full-on attack. Ever since her parents died, she had dealt with anxiety. It didn't help that she had no pressing deadlines at work to distract her. She'd finished her last two freelance projects the week before. Since she couldn't escape into her work, it was a perfect time to go house hunting.

The howl of wind whistling through her windows reminded her of the approaching storm. Hopefully Cassie had some time for her that morning; otherwise they'd have to wait a few days. Which wasn't good. Emma needed a project, now!

Dialing Cassie's number while she descended the stairs to the kitchen, she glanced outside at the cloud cover and tree branches, whipping to and fro.

"This is Cassie Vincent. I'm sorry I'm either away from my phone or with a client. If you'll leave a message I'll call—"

Emma pushed the End Call button as she noticed her front porch rug tumble across the lawn toward the street.

"Oh great!" she exclaimed yanking open the front door. Holding her robe together with one hand, she burst onto the porch and stumbled against the force of the wind.

Forging ahead with her rescue mission, she ran to catch up with the rug that was in motion again, and after two failed attempts at grabbing it, she pounced on it like a cat on a windup mouse.

"Gotcha!" She brought the rug inside until the storm blew over.

Needing something warm to drink, she filled a mug with water and put it in the microwave then found the packet of hot chocolate with marshmallows.

Popping two pieces of whole grain bread into the toaster, she gazed out the window.

By the time she settled in front of her computer with her mug of cocoa and toast with raspberry jam, she had managed to calm down. Her e-mail in-box was full, and she took the next thirty minutes responding, deleting, or making notes of matters that needed her attention.

The vibration of her phone on the counter caught her attention. Hoping it was Landon, she rushed to see who had texted her.

"Margaret." Regretting that she'd helped the woman learn how to text, she read the message.

My dearest daughter-in-law, could you find time to call? I desperately need your help today.

Ugh! What in the world did this woman want from her, and what was with this *dearest* business? There wasn't an ounce of sincerity behind it. She stopped for a moment, remembering the movie about Joan Crawford, *Mommie Dearest.* She laughed out loud when she had the wicked thought to text back, *Margaret Dearest.* While her son had been alive, Margaret had barely given Emma the time of day, but now that he was gone, Margaret wouldn't leave her alone.

Closing her eyes to gather her strength, she pulled in a deep breath and let it out slowly. *Just get it over with*, she told herself. The woman was old and alone and supposedly sickly. Emma still felt an obligation to her.

She lifted her phone to dial, then paused. The wind had died down some and sun had broken through the clouds. At least the day was improving.

"Fine!" she exclaimed as she pressed the buttons to make the call, "but I'm not going over. I have too much to do today." Then she released a frustrated sigh, knowing that was a lie. After the airport, she didn't have anything to do that day, unless Cassie called.

Praying Margaret didn't pick up so she could just leave a message and get credit for at least trying, she began to breathe easier after the third ring, knowing the next sound she heard would be the voice mail telling her to leave a message.

"Emma, my dear, is that you?"

Emma stifled a laugh, which ended up sounding like a sneeze.

"Bless you," Margaret said. "Are you coming down with a cold?"

Emma clamped her lips together to prevent her from responding with *Margaret Dearest*. She rolled her eyes and forced her voice to be pleasant. "Hello, Margaret. How are you?"

"I'm as well as can be expected, I suppose. These doctors keep trying to convince me that I have ten years left in this old body, but I know they are just full of bull-pucky."

Emma laughed. "Why do you say that?"

"I just know, inside. There's not much time left. That's why I called."

"You called to tell me you don't have much time left?"

"I called to see if you had some time today to come over. There's something very, very important I've been needing to do, and I want to take care of it before the weather gets bad and winter sets in."

"What is it?"

"I'd rather wait and tell you when you get here. Can you be here at noon?"

What if the old woman was right? What if she did pass away soon? Emma needed to realize that someday Margaret would be gone.

She could swing by after she took Landon to the airport, and while she was out, she could grab a few groceries. "Yes, of course I can be there."

"Oh, thank you, sweetie. You've made me so happy. Drive safely."

Emma told her good-bye then forced herself to get showered. Consulting the weather app on her phone, she decided to wear layers since the temperature was dropping as the cold front moved in. She put on a long-sleeved, cream-colored T-shirt and a bronze-brown cardigan. Wrapping a brown and rust plaid scarf around her neck, she added a pair of golden rhinestone hoop earrings and pulled on her brown leather riding boots over her slim-cut jeans. She doubted Margaret would approve.

Margaret was from the East coast, born and bred, and she preferred a classic wardrobe of tan tailored trousers, sweater sets, and pearls.

Emma didn't even own a set of pearls, fake or otherwise. It wasn't her style, which again was part of the reason Margaret never accepted her.

After she got dressed, she straightened the kitchen and was about to start a load of laundry when Jess called her.

"Hey girl, whatcha doin'?"

"Hi. Just waiting for Landon to pick me up so I can take him to the airport. Totally not looking forward to it."

"That's why I called. Want to go to lunch, maybe do a little shopping? Might help get your mind off your hunka-hunka burning love."

Emma laughed. "I'd love to, but it will have to be a little later. My ex-mother-in-law needs me to stop by after I drop off Landon."

"It's my day off, so I'm flexible. Call me when you're leaving her, and we can meet somewhere. Although I have to warn you, I'm in the mood for sushi. Or chicken fingers. I can't decide yet. It's still too early in the morning."

"Whatever you decide sounds good."

"Oh, before I forget, can you tell me the name of your realtor? I have a friend at work who wants to find a place closer to the office and wants to put their house up for sale and find something else."

"Sure. Her name is Cassie Vincent. She's awesome."

"Cassie Vincent?"

"Yeah, you know her?"

"Did she grow up in Seattle?"

"I'm pretty sure she did."

"Did she go to Garfield High School?"

"I don't know, Jess."

"Is she tall, blonde, athletic build, the cheerleader type?"

"Um, I guess you could say that. Why?"

"I'll find someone else," Jess said abruptly.

"What? Wait, I don't understand. Cassie's awesome. She's a great realtor and a good friend."

She heard Jess's frustrated sigh over the phone.

"Jess, what's going on?"

"Well, the fact is she's the reason I'm not married and don't have kids by now."

"I'm sorry, what?"

"I know that sounds harsh, but it's true. I started dating a guy named Sean Baxter my junior year of high school. After one date we both knew we'd get married someday. He was on the basketball team, and I was his biggest fan. We were two of the few Mormons in our school, so it was insane that we not only liked each other but fell in love. I mean, it seemed like heaven had it all planned out. Even our parents were excited about us getting married, after his mission, of course.

"And then, Cassie moved in the end of junior year. She made it just in time for cheer tryouts. She was from California, so she was this beautiful, tan, leggy blonde, who not only made the cheer squad but also was put in as head cheerleader. All the boys fell in love with her. She had everything. And, she was LDS."

Emma knew where she was going with her story.

"It didn't take long for things to change. She knew Sean and I were dating, but that didn't stop her. In her bubbly, outgoing way, she managed to steal Sean right out from under me. I guess in her defense, he didn't put up much of a fight. The first Sunday she came to church and paid attention to him, he started losing interest; he couldn't resist her. I think it would have been easier to accept had he at least broken up with me first then started to date her. I guess he thought he'd let me down easy and keep going out with me, but I found out later that after our dates he'd drop me off and go out with her. I would have thought more of her if she would have told him to end things with me first."

Emma had never heard the edge of pain in Jess's voice before. Jess was always so positive and upbeat.

When Emma didn't say anything, Jess said, "I'm sorry. TMI, right?"

"I just don't know what to say. Cassie is such a great person and friend. Yes, she's gorgeous and outgoing, but she is very professional and respectful. I'm not the same person I was in high school. Maybe she's changed."

"Maybe. They dated until he went on his mission, and the day after he left she was with another guy. And the funny thing is, Sean wrote me from his mission, but I had no interest in him after that."

"I'm really sorry you got hurt, Jess."

"I'm over it, really, but I just haven't thought about Cassie for years. Hearing her name brought back some painful memories."

"I understand. I think most people's first loves are hard to get over."

"Thanks for listening and understanding. I'll see you soon, and I promise I'll cheer you up, not the other way around. Also, I'm thinking Italian now. Pasta sounds kind of good."

"Sounds like you're hungry. Maybe you need something to eat now."

"Hey, maybe you're right. I only had a few bites of toast before I went to my yoga class."

"Oh, one last thing," Emma remembered. "Didn't you say you met with a therapist when you were having anxiety problems?"

"I did—her name was Lisa James. She's awesome. She helped me a lot."

"I think I'll make an appointment."

"You should, Em. I know it would be good for you."

Emma knew it was time to face the fears that held her back in her life. Landon loved her in spite of them, but she wanted to be strong and in charge of her life when they got married.

Emma's phone buzzed, indicating an incoming text. The two women said good-bye, and Emma checked her messages. Landon was just around the corner. It was time for him to leave.

As he pulled in the driveway, she fought the tears that threatened. It wasn't going to make it easier on either of them if she got emotional.

The ride to the airport was quiet. They shared small talk, but there was really nothing to say. The last thing she wanted was for him to go. The month ahead loomed like a prison sentence.

"Cell phone service will be sketchy, but I should be able to find Internet each day. We can video chat sometimes too."

She nodded.

"Hey," he reached for her hand. "I'll be home before you know it."

Trying to be pleasant, she agreed with him and pointed out a new Mexican restaurant that would be opening up in the area while he was gone.

Promising to take her when he got home, he followed the exit sign indicating that they were almost to the airport.

"So, do you and Cassie have plans to get together today?" he asked.

"I left a message for her, but she hasn't returned my call. I seem to remember her saying something about some sales meetings or something, so hopefully after that she'll call me."

"I hope so. It would be great to find something soon, especially with it being a fixer-upper. We'll want plenty of time to work on it."

"If we don't get together today, I have a light schedule the rest of the week, so I'm sure we'll get together. I have to run and see Margaret, then I'm going to lunch with Jess. Remind me when we talk later to tell you something Jess told me."

"Oh? Sounds interesting. I will. It's nice of you to spend time with Margaret. I'm sure she appreciates it more than she says."

"I doubt it. She just expects everyone to jump when she needs anything. I just hope she understands that things are going to change after we get married."

"Maybe that's why she's being so demanding right now. She knows that after we're married it won't be the same."

Emma hadn't thought about that before. "You could be right."

"At least you have lunch with Jess to look forward to. I gotta ask, though, how does someone who loves to eat so much stay so thin?"

Emma laughed out loud. "Don't think I haven't wondered the same thing, and that I haven't asked. She's got this freakishly high metabolism. No surprise though, since she's hyper pretty much all the time."

"I've noticed. I sat next to her on the stand at church when we both gave talks, and she was fidgeting the entire time."

"That's part of the reason I love being around her. Her energy is—"

Her sentence was cut short when Landon pulled up to the curb in front of the Delta terminal. They were there.

Emma's thoughts quickly evaporated, replaced by sadness and fear.

"There are cars behind us; we'd better hurry," he said.

They hugged once before getting out of the car, then again after he got his bag out of the trunk.

"I'll talk to you soon," he said.

She gave him a brave, happy smile.

"I won't forget the Swiss chocolate."

"All I need is you and chocolate, and I'm good."

"You can count on me. I won't come back without it."

They looked at each other for a moment then he glanced at his watch. "Sorry, sweetie. I'd better get going."

"Okay," she said, reaching up for a final hug.

He kissed her on the forehead then grabbed the handle of his rolling suitcase and was off.

Emma stood, watching him walk into the terminal, the pain in her heart deepening with every footstep that took him away from her.

Tears spilled onto her cheeks, and the stiff wind blew them dry.

The honk of a horn startled her. People were waiting for her to move so they could drop their own passengers.

Hurrying around the SUV, she jumped into the driver's seat and, through blurred vision, pulled into the lane of traffic.

Gripping the steering wheel with both hands, she pushed her sadness aside while she maneuvered the SUV away from the busy airport. Driving the back roads all the way home would take forever. She had no choice but to head up the on-ramp and merge onto the busy freeway. A sudden realization dawned on her. Her new life ahead—with marriage and someday a family—was not going to allow her to stay inside the risk-free zone she'd created for herself. Things that concerned or frightened her wouldn't fit inside her cocoon of safety. Whether she wanted to or not, it was time to step outside into the real world.

* * *

The care center where Margaret lived was a beautiful facility with a resort feel to it. The grounds were impeccable; the Tuscan design and décor created a warm, elegant atmosphere. It was the best facility around; Margaret wouldn't have considered anything less.

Finding a secluded spot toward the back of the parking lot, Emma parked Landon's SUV. Parking lots were notorious for dings, and she was willing to do anything she had to so she could avoid one.

A gust of bitter cold wind greeted her as she stepped out of the car. Glad she wore her down-filled, thigh-length parka, she double-checked that the car was locked then hurried toward the large building that had become her mother-in-law's new home.

Her phone buzzed, and she looked to see a new text from Jess.

Can you still do lunch at noon? I can do 12:30 too if that's better. How do you feel about Thai? Just found a new restaurant that looks fabulous, right next to a new cupcake place.

Emma responded that anything was good with her and that she'd text when she was done at the care center.

Why don't we plan on 12:30 then, just to be safe.

Emma smiled. Jess was a bit of a "control freak," but Emma actually wished she were a little more like Jess sometimes. Her friend was high energy, high efficiency, high intensity. Granted, Jess could get weird about cleaning and organizing, especially when she was in charge of anything, but the end result was usually impressive and spectacular. They served on the Relief Society night meeting committee together, and Emma honestly had to leave the room after Jess rearranged the chairs at a Relief Society birthday party banquet for the fourth time. And then there was that time they were in charge of decorations for the young adult stake Valentine's dance. After decorating and redecorating all day, Emma didn't even want to go to the dance. Of course, the event turned out beautifully and was a huge success, but Emma never wanted to see another Pinterest post in her life.

She ascended the steps into the building, dread growing inside her. These visits never went well and usually ended up with Emma having to bite her tongue and needing Advil. No one ever won against Margaret; it wasn't even worth the fight.

Pausing just outside the front door, she took several breaths to prepare herself for the visit. Spending time with Margaret was exhausting. She reminded herself of the fact that her mother-in-law had no other family around, except a sister on the East coast. It made Emma feel badly that she wasn't better about visiting Margaret. Without her friends to keep her company while Landon was gone, Emma too would feel very lonely. The woman probably felt desperate to have someone to spend time with. Emma knew she had an obligation to her former mother-in-law, but she wasn't used to their new relationship now that Jonathan was gone. Her mother-in-law had wanted nothing to do with her when he was alive, and now that he was gone, she couldn't get enough of her. Margaret had never hidden her feelings about Emma not being the right girl or good enough for her son, and she had rarely included Emma in any part of her life. This chummy attitude was hard to adjust to, even though Margaret still treated her like she was on a lower social level.

Emma pulled the door open and forced herself to walk inside. Her boots clicked on the shiny linoleum as she walked toward the check-in desk. Part of the reason she dreaded the visits was that the two women had nothing to talk about and Margaret was so critical of her.

That pretty much sucked the fun out of their visits within the first ten minutes. With Jonathan gone they had nothing in common.

The girl at the front desk was new. Emma signed the registry then started toward her mother-in-law's room.

"She's very excited about today," the girl said.

"Oh," Emma gave her a smile, "that's nice to hear." Emma felt a twinge of guilt nudge her. Was Margaret so lonely she told the whole staff when her daughter-in-law was coming to visit?

She tapped on the door to Margaret's room before she went in.

"Emma, is that you? Come in, dear."

Emma pushed the door open and peeked inside.

Margaret was sitting in her wheelchair, next to the window. A beautiful hand-stitched quilt covered her legs, and she wore a thick gray sweater.

"We're in for a winter storm. I can feel it in my bones." The woman continued to stare out the window.

"That's what I hear. It's been so beautiful lately I almost forgot it was winter."

Emma walked over to the woman and leaned over to give her a hug. Margaret stiffened at her touch, like she always did.

"How are you feeling?" Emma asked, sitting in a chair close by.

"I've been fighting this cough for a few days. I'm convinced I have pneumonia, but they did a chest x-ray and said my lungs are clear. I guess I can't argue with that, but with all my years in nursing, as well as having pneumonia three times myself, I think I know how it feels." She finally looked at Emma, pausing to give Emma a chance to speak.

"I could talk to the nurse for you," Emma suggested. "I'm sure they don't want you going untreated if you have pneu—"

"No!" she exclaimed. "I mean, thank you, but that's not necessary. I'm sure they are doing their best. It's just that I don't think they understand how fast it can come on. I just don't think I'd survive another bout with it."

"You sure you don't want me to ask them?"

"No. I don't want to say anything that might get in the way of my outing. It's the only thing keeping me sane."

Outing? What outing?

Emma didn't ask but nodded her head and made the appropriate noises to show she was agreeing with her, whether she did or not. This made their conversations and their visits go much easier. Emma had learned at the beginning of her marriage that Margaret never backed down and never held back her opinion. Someone like Cassie would have spoken up and confronted the woman. Cassie would never be a doormat. Emma wasn't proud of it, but that's exactly how she felt with Margaret.

"You look a little peaked yourself, dear. Aren't you sleeping well?" Margaret peered at her with an inspecting eye.

"Actually I'm sleeping wonderfully." That wasn't exactly true. She wouldn't admit it to Margaret though. Emma was worried about Landon's trip, and it was keeping her up at night. Margaret neither fully understood the deep-rooted fear of air travel, nor did she approve of Emma marrying Landon. She never came out and said it, but she didn't have to; her condescending, subtle, passive-aggressive remarks left no doubt.

"Did you have one of your photo shoots outside today before you came?"

Emma tilted her head while processing the question. Then she realized that Margaret was launching a disapproving comment on her outfit and her hair. "No, just trying to stay warm and comfortable." She'd quit letting Margaret's digs get to her. She never looked right or dressed right as far as Margaret was concerned.

"I see. You've let your hair grow."

Forcing a pleasant response, Emma said, "I have. I like it longer so I can pull it back in a ponytail."

Margaret didn't reply, but Emma knew the woman didn't approve. Jonathan was very adamant about Emma wearing her hair in a chin-length bob. At first, he'd talked her into it because it would bring out her eyes and complement her jawline. After a year of marriage, though, when she'd decided to grow it out, Jonathan had told her she needed to keep it short, in a style that befit the wife of a doctor. Of course, she'd wanted to please him and keep him happy, so she dressed and altered her appearance according to his wishes. She helped his image, allowed him to play the part in the community that was expected of him, but underneath his name tag and lab coat was a completely different person.

It was never spoken of or addressed so it didn't exist—at least that was the game they all played.

The two women didn't say anything for a few minutes. Emma wondered how long she needed to wait before she could end the visit without Margaret objecting to her "leaving so soon." And then whatever outing Margaret was talking about would be forgotten.

Emma's gaze rested on a Bible on the woman's nightstand. It was open, like someone had recently been reading it. Margaret's eyes followed her gaze. Then she asked, "Do Mormons read the Bible?"

Emma looked at her mother-in-law with surprise. Was she serious? "Yes, we study it a great deal."

"Oh, I didn't realize. I thought with your Mormon Bible you didn't bother with the real one."

Nothing would have pleased Emma more than to correct her mother-in-law and give her an explanation of the Book of Mormon, its origin, and how members of her faith used both of the sets of scriptures to study the life and teachings of Christ. She'd tried to explain this once before but the discussion led to Margaret expressing concern for Emma being fooled by this new husband-to-be of hers. Margaret was a very smart woman; she just played like she didn't know so she could reel Emma into one of her lectures on why she was getting married too soon and that she didn't know enough about Landon to really be safe.

Emma wasn't up to the fight, nor was it worth it to even step into the ring. Margaret could verbally spar with anyone and never backed down. When the punches weren't focused on her, Emma actually was impressed with Margaret's debate skills. She would have made a marvelous prosecutor.

However, the most exhausting part of their relationship was that the woman could never be pleased and didn't have the capacity to let go of the pain caused by the death of her husband seven years earlier to a fatal heart attack and, more recently, her son.

"I've been reading a great deal in the scriptures lately. Seems like a good idea, since it won't be long before I meet my Maker."

Emma tried to assure her she had a lot of years ahead of her, but Margaret ignored her comment and went on. "I suppose, then, that you are familiar with the story of Ruth and Naomi?"

"Yes, I am."

"I've been studying it for some time now."

She could tell Margaret had more to say, so Emma remained silent. This was Margaret's first real mention that showed any interest in religion, other than to slam the LDS Church any chance she could.

"Our situation is not so different, is it?" Margaret asked.

"Oh?"

"Naomi, the older woman losing her son, and her daughter-in-law refusing to leave her side and staying with her to take care of her."

"Yes, I guess in some ways it is similar." Emma wasn't comfortable with where this was going. Surely Margaret wasn't suggesting Emma take her in to care for her.

"Yet, there is a difference. Quite a big one."

"What's that, Margaret?"

"Naomi depended upon her daughter-in-law to provide for her. I am anything but poor. In fact, Emma, that is one of the reasons I wanted you to come over today."

Emma was confused, but part of her was very interested in what Margaret was getting at.

"Dear, you know you are my only close family now. Even my sister and I have grown distant and rarely speak. She was always jealous that I married well and was a woman of influence in the community. This strained our relationship greatly." She sighed and placed her thin, blue-veined hand on her chest.

This was new information to Emma. Knowledge of her mother-in-law's relatives and past had always been kept from her.

"You probably have figured out what I'm getting at. But you need to know that when I pass away, I will be leaving . . . everything I have . . . to you."

Margaret peered into her face, her gaze circling Emma's expression, as if trying to read her thoughts.

Stunned and immediately uncomfortable with the obligations that would be connected with receiving "everything" Margaret had, Emma didn't know what to say.

"Well?" Margaret prompted, obviously dissatisfied with Emma's reaction.

"Margaret, I honestly don't know what to say. I need to tell you though, I'm not really comfortable—"

Margaret held up her hand to stop her.

"But—"

"You must allow me to do this. It is the only way I will leave this earth in peace. You have shown your devotion to me, and I want to reward you."

Not sure if she was allowed to talk, Emma held her tongue. Besides, she still didn't know what to say or what to think. She knew Margaret. There had to be strings attached. Big, thick, binding strings, like webs of a spider, wrapping around her, tighter and tighter.

"Margaret, I really can't accept—"

"However . . ."

Ah, here it comes. It's her way or no way. I knew there was a catch.

"There is something very important I need to do, while I can still get around, and you are the only one who can help me."

Unsure of where this was going, afraid to ask, Emma swallowed then forced herself to say the words. "What's that Margaret?"

"I need you to take me to our cabin. I need to go just one last time."

Emma had never been to the family cabin. Jonathan had spoken of it occasionally and had even wanted to spend time there during the summer, but he'd never been able to break away from work long enough for them to spend a weekend. She had known better than to push him. He had inherited his mother's tendency to control and demand her life. She hated the fact that she'd lost her backbone, but standing up to him just hadn't been worth it. She'd loved Jonathan at one time, but she didn't miss having him in her life.

"I know how busy you are with your career and your fiancé and your wedding plans and that it's a lot to ask, but it would mean the world to me. I understand the weather is going to turn bad this week, and once the snow falls, they close the roads until spring. I just don't dare wait much longer. I don't even know if I'll be around by then."

Did Margaret want to go today? Right now?

"I know you aren't a fan of driving on the freeway, but it's a lovely drive and we wouldn't have to stay long."

She expected Emma to drop everything and drive her to the family cabin.

"Of course, I understand if you have pressing matters to take care of."

There it was . . . the guilt trip.

Was this some kind of test to see if Emma would put Margaret's needs above her own? Not to mention that, yes, Emma did have plans. She was going to lunch with Jess. Of course, Jess would understand if she cancelled, but that was beside the point. She didn't want to spend an entire afternoon with the woman. As far as she was concerned, she'd overstayed her required time as it was.

"I have already met with my lawyer, and he has drawn up the necessary papers to change my will. Except for this final loose end at the cabin, I will have all my affairs in order. I hate to spring this on you last minute, but you are really the only one who can do this with me. It affects you directly, I'm afraid. Is there any way you could help me out, dear?"

Drat! In her mind Emma was screaming her true feelings. She would sooner have a root canal than help Margaret out, but darn it, the woman was leaving her entire estate, all of her assets, to her. An afternoon with her wasn't too much to ask in return. Was it?

"Today is fine." Emma couldn't infuse any enthusiasm into her words. She was sincere, but she wasn't happy about it.

The woman's eyes opened wide with apparent surprise. "Well, isn't that lovely. I'm so glad you can get away." The woman pointed to a floral print oversized bag. "If you'll get my bag, we can leave."

How did this woman manage to orchestrate things so beautifully? Not only had Emma played right into her hands, but the woman had everything all planned out, knowing she could get Emma to acquiesce.

"Don't we need to get permission to leave?"

"Not at all, dear. I already mentioned I would be leaving today. They all know. Outings are encouraged. It's good for us to have a change of scenery, get some fresh air. This is assisted living, dear. I'm not in prison."

Emma wondered if that was what the front desk girl had been referring to when she mentioned how excited Margaret was for the day. She was so amazed by the woman's talent to manipulate everyone around her that she actually felt like clapping. She was truly in the presence of a master.

Something inside of her told her to ask one of the nurses if it was okay to take Margaret from the facility, but she knew that would set off Margaret, and she didn't want to cause a scene. So she pushed the thought out of her head and helped the woman gather her things.

Hooking the large bag over one of the handles on the back of Margaret's wheelchair, Emma began pushing the chair. Swells of anger churned inside of her. Had this been an isolated occurrence she might not have been so bothered. But this wasn't the first time Emma had felt this way, nor would it be the last. The theme ran long and strong throughout her marriage to Jonathan. Aside from the fact that Jonathan had been a workaholic and traveled constantly, leaving her for days, sometimes weeks at a time, most likely vacationing with one of his many female friends, and had been controlling and often demeaning, the greatest source of contention in their marriage had been his relationship with his mother. When she called, he went running like a scared puppy. It didn't matter if it was interrupting a special dinner, a movie, or in the middle of the night. He went running back to her. And after he passed away, Emma somehow got caught up in Margaret's far-reaching tentacles.

Her mother-in-law was prattling on about some articles, awards, and achievements from Jonathan's childhood and youth, but Emma was only half listening. All she could think about was that once she was married, things had to change. She couldn't be leaving Landon to tend to her mother-in-law's every need. Landon had mentioned several times about moving to the East coast, since so much of his business was in Europe. It would make sense to shave five hours off his flights by moving. She loved Seattle, it was home, but moving away and being on their own, suddenly proved very appealing.

Managing to push Margaret and her abundance of belongings through the door of her room, Emma prayed for strength as she anticipated the upcoming hours ahead. The two women had nothing to talk about. It was going to be a long afternoon.

"Turn left at this next corner. We can go out the side door," Margaret instructed as they traveled down the hallway. "I really don't want to run into any of those dim-witted nurses, or heaven forbid, Dr. Fallon."

"Why not?" Emma followed directions but worried that maybe Margaret needed final clearance to leave for the afternoon.

"They treat me like a child. I know as much about medicine as all of them combined, yet they refuse to listen to me. So infuriating!"

"Are you sure—"

"Please, just do as I ask," Margaret demanded then she began coughing.

"Margaret!" Emma panicked. Maybe leaving wasn't a good idea.

Margaret waved away Emma's concern. "Please, let's just get out of here!"

AGAINST HER BETTER JUDGMENT, EMMA pushed the wheelchair forward, exiting the building from a side entrance that led to the back of the building, where Landon's car was parked. Her promise to Landon of becoming more feisty rang hollow in her memory. Why couldn't she just say she wasn't comfortable taking Margaret away from the center and that she was even more nervous to drive up to the cabin?

With her coughing spasm under control, Margaret rested a hand on her chest and exclaimed, "Fresh air! That's just what I need. I feel better already."

Just do it! Say something, she told herself. She stopped pushing the wheelchair. "Margaret, I'm a little worried—"

Margaret turned her head and shot Emma a look that stopped her from uttering another word. The woman wouldn't be denied. She didn't care about any of Emma's concerns or fears.

"We need to hurry," Margaret told her. "It gets dark early."

"But—"

"Emma, I'm not sure I'm making myself clear. We have to do this today, and we have to go now!"

Emma shut her eyes and fought the surge of anger building inside of her. She wasn't just angry with Margaret; she was mad at herself for being such a coward.

She gave the wheelchair a shove, catching Margaret off guard.

Expecting Margaret to blast her with further criticism and commands, Emma was surprised when nothing came.

Just get it over with. She had to learn how to avoid situations like this in the future. And if she got in trouble for taking Margaret when she wasn't supposed to, maybe they wouldn't let Emma take her again. That would be okay.

"Why, thank you, dear," Margaret said when Emma helped her into the passenger's seat. Her insincere endearments were getting old because there was nothing loving or caring about her actions. "This is a nice vehicle. That fiancé of yours must make a better living than I gave him credit for."

What was Emma supposed to say to a comment like that? The woman had offended her so often, she didn't bother rising to the bait any longer. It just wasn't worth it, and she didn't want to give Margaret the satisfaction of knowing she got to her.

Emma folded the wheelchair and lifted it into the back of the vehicle, then climbed inside.

"So, I'm not exactly sure which direction I'm going." She started the engine, making a mental note to text Jess. Margaret was so consuming and demanding it was difficult to even get a quick text in sideways.

"Once we get on the freeway, I'll show you which exit to take. It's quite simple and a lovely drive."

Again Emma wanted to kick herself for letting this outing get this far. She didn't want to drive up to the cabin, she didn't want to go anywhere with Margaret, and she hadn't even had a chance to check her phone to see if Landon had texted her that he was getting on his flight like he usually did.

Well, Margaret would just have to wait. She checked her phone, and sure enough, she had a message from Landon telling her he was boarding his flight and would let her know when they got into Denver. She sent him a quick text telling him she loved him and hoped he had a good flight then added a couple of red kissy lip emojis.

She had also missed a call and a text from Jess.

"Shoot!" she exclaimed. There was no way she was going to make it by twelve thirty.

"Is there a problem? We really ought to get going." Margaret turned and looked back at the facility.

"I just have to let my friend know I can't make it for lunch."

It made her mad that Margaret didn't seem bothered by the fact that she had interrupted Emma's plans for the day. *Don't blame Margaret. It's your own fault, you big coward*, she told herself.

She let Jess know that something had come up and she was sorry but she couldn't make it for lunch. She added, *Send the code in four hours.*

She hid her smile, knowing that if Margaret found out what she was doing, the woman would be furious. She and Jess had a plan to help each other whenever they needed to get out of a bad situation, whether it was a date, an awkward party, or any sort of undesirable situation. One would sent a text or call and say there was an emergency or some sort of appointment they had forgotten about, giving the other an excuse to leave. Emma allowed for one hour up to the cabin, two hours there, and one hour back. That was plenty of time to take care of whatever Margaret needed to take care of.

Emma put her phone down and started the engine. She looked over at Margaret, who was glaring at her. She opened her mouth to apologize but then decided not to. There was nothing to be sorry for.

Dreading everything about the trip, Emma pulled onto the main road that led toward the interstate. Margaret told her which direction to go, and without a backwards glance, they were off to the cabin.

A strong headwind kept Emma's focus locked on the roads. She wondered how soon the storm was supposed to hit. Without asking if Margaret minded, Emma turned on the radio to try and catch a weather report.

". . . unloading snow and ice along a broad west-to-east swath from the Rocky Mountains to the Midwest. Sustained winds, severe drops in temperature, and heavy precipitation are expected to continue for the next twenty-four hours. This is creating hazardous driving conditions on several major highways and forcing the closure of many major aiports. Stay tuned as we get more details."

An ad for a local car dealership blasted, and Emma quickly lowered the volume. The plane carrying Landon was flying straight into the storm.

"So tell me, how is your photography business going?"

The last thing Emma felt like doing was making conversation with Margaret. "It's keeping me busy. Today's one of the few days I didn't have a shoot. The rest of my week is booked solid."

"Is that so? And how are wedding preparations going?"

"Good," she said, straining to hear if the weather had come back on. "We've gotten a lot of it done."

"Tell me about your wedding dress. Please tell me you found something more suitable to your body type than that concoction you wore when you married my son."

Emma's first wedding dress was simple and demure. A satin, boat-necked creation that fit at the waist then followed the curve of her hip and billowed out around the knees, with an underskirt of tulle in gathered layers. To her it was exquisite; to Margaret it was a concoction. Sheesh! "Well, I saw this dress in a magazine that was made from this gorgeous antique lace and pearls. It's very vintage and feminine, and my fiancé—"

"I'm really glad we have a little time ourselves while we're driving," Margaret interrupted. "There is something I need to say to you."

Emma gripped the steering wheel tightly and wondered how she was supposed to survive an entire afternoon with Margaret. What did Margaret possibly have to say to her? She never knew what to expect from this woman; all she knew was that most of the time it wasn't good.

"I've been trying to get my affairs in order, since my days are numbered, and I've needed to update my will since Jonathan passed away." She cleared her throat a few times then coughed, covering her mouth with a tissue.

The way Margaret talked you would think she had one foot in the grave, but Emma gathered, from talking with doctors that for a woman her age she was in relatively good health. "Oh Margaret, you are going to around for a long, long time," Emma said absently as she listened for more information about that winter storm. But the reporter was rambling on about some sort of tax reform bill.

"No, dear. I can't explain it, but a person knows when it's time to start tying up loose ends and making things right. And I feel like there are a few things I would like to say to you, while I can."

"No, Margaret, really, everything is good with us."

It was too late for a heart-to-heart. Nothing the woman said at this point could undo the years of disappointment and criticism.

"That's sweet of you, but I can't rest in peace until I speak my mind."

"Maybe some things are best left alone." Emma really didn't want things to get more awkward. She did not want to have some deep conversation with the woman.

Margaret took a deep breath and sighed wearily. Emma glanced over at her then looked back at the road and smiled. Margaret had a flair for the dramatic.

"Oh, this is our exit. You'll follow the signs toward Mount Baker."

Glad they were finally getting off the interstate—thankfully it hadn't been too congested—Emma took the exit.

"What I need to tell you is important," Margaret said. "Would you mind turning off the radio?"

"I'd like to hear if there are any updates on the storm. Landon's flight is heading that direction."

She turned up the volume, but the reporter was covering a story about some NBA basketball game. Earlier there seemed to be such concern about the storm, why weren't they coming back to it?

"Just stay on this road a few more miles," Margaret instructed.

"I can't believe I never came here with Jonathan. He mentioned it once, but it never came up again. I kind of forgot about it."

"We spent a lot of time there when he was young, but as he grew up and got busy with friends and sports, it was harder to get away. Then college took him back East, and just after he returned home to start his practice here, Charles died. After that it just wasn't a priority. We've neglected it badly, I'm afraid."

The landscape slowly changed, becoming mountainous and thickly forested. The road had become two lanes, winding higher and deeper into the mountains.

Emma was about to call one of her friends to see if possibly they could find out about the storm when the traffic and weather report finally came on.

The reporter seemed to talk about weather everywhere but the Denver area. Finally, before going to the break, he said, "The strength of this storm system seems to have increased, with a possible accumulation of twelve to fourteen inches over the next forty-eight hours. Authorities are asking people to stay off the roads. Schools have been closed, and we're seeing power outages in some areas of Denver from the high winds accompanying the storm system. "

"You said your fiancé is flying to Denver right now?" Margaret asked.

Emma couldn't answer. She nodded her head.

"I'm sure he'll be fine. They usually avert planes if it's not safe to fly in the area. Although this storm sounds like it's moving pretty fast. Maybe they didn't have time to change course."

Was she serious? Why would she say that? Emma was worried enough without Margaret giving voice to her fears.

"I'm sorry, dear. I don't mean to make you worry. I'm sure he'll be fine."

The last person Emma wanted to be around right now was Margaret. Emma's level of concern was reaching the point of panic, and she needed to be home, not up in the mountains. "Margaret, I'm sorry, but we need to go back. I'm really worried. Besides, didn't you hear, we have an Arctic front heading our way. We could be in for snow ourselves. We shouldn't be up here."

"It's only ten minutes from here," Margaret said. "Could we just go in, grab what I need, then leave?"

Emma felt like she was going to leave indents in the steering wheel she was gripping it so hard.

"Fine, but we need to hurry," she snapped. She didn't even look at the woman. Instead, she pressed on the gas to get them there quicker. The sooner they got there, the sooner they could leave.

After a few seconds of silence, Margaret said, "Thank you for bringing me today. You've been such a dear to come whenever I've called, and I appreciate your devotion and concern. You really are the only person I have in my life who I can count on and really understands how I feel."

Inside Emma was forming responses and fighting the urge to scream them.

"I don't know what I'd do without you."

"What about your sister?"

"That ungrateful snit?" Margaret gave a huff and folded her arms. "She missed Jonathan's funeral for heaven's sake!"

Emma had only met Margaret's sister once, when she and Jonathan got married. She had seemed like a warm and gracious woman.

"As long as I have you I don't need anyone else," Margaret said. "I know that we haven't always gotten along or seen eye to eye, but I think of you as my own daughter. And I apologize for anything I've done that might have hurt you or caused you pain."

As insincere as the apology was, Emma was surprised by Margaret's words. This was strange behavior for the woman. Margaret had never admitted she was wrong. Ever.

"Thank you, Margaret. I don't know what to say."

"I realize I've been hard on you. Frankly, darling, it wouldn't have mattered who married my son; no one would have been good enough for him in my eyes. But you were devoted and loving to him, and you made him very happy. It was hard to have someone take my place in his life, and I realize I didn't make it easy for you, but you never caved. You are a strong, remarkable woman, and I'm grateful to have you in my life."

Emma was on the brink of freaking out. Was Margaret on some sort of personality altering drug? If so, she liked it.

"I know I took Jonathan away at times when I needed help, and I hope that didn't cause too much trouble. He was always so devoted to drop everything and come when I called."

At times it seemed she was making up excuses so she could call and have him come to the house to spend time with her. She never asked for Emma to join them, just her son. Emma didn't mind. Anytime she could avoid Margaret's biting remarks and criticism, she did it.

"Anyway," her mother-in-law continued, sniffing into her tissue. "Thank you for everything. You have proven yourself in my eyes."

Wait, did she actually mean what she was saying? Emma detected a note of uncharacteristic sincerity underlining the woman's words. "Wow, thank you, Margaret," Emma answered. "I always had hoped we could be close."

"I want that also," she said. "Yes, that is my wish as well."

The timing wasn't exactly the best. Just as Emma was ready to remarry and move on with her life, Margaret was deciding to be nice? She didn't know what to make of it.

Emma slowed as they came to a fork in the road.

"Stay to the left. It's not much farther. I can't wait to show it to you. It really is heaven on earth."

The bumpy, dirt road kicked up dust as they traveled deeper into the forest. With all the twists and turns, Emma wasn't sure which direction they were going anymore. Of course, it wasn't too hard for her to get turned around. She got lost in a shopping mall.

"Oh, we turn right here," Margaret said.

Following the dirt road splitting off from the main road, Emma slowed down the vehicle and began driving up the unpaved road into the trees.

"In the winter when we came we would have to snowmobile into the cabin. It was my favorite place to come because it was the only way we could really escape the city, the patients, and the telephones." She coughed several times then drew in several ragged breaths.

"Everything okay?" Emma asked, not liking the tight sound of the cough.

It took another moment for Margaret to calm her cough. "It just hits me all of a sudden like that."

"I'm a little worried to have you so far away from medical care."

"I'm fine. Don't forget, I'm a nurse. I have my medications with me, and I have you. That's all I need."

The bumpy off-road conditions forced Emma to slow the vehicle down to a crawl. She didn't want to damage Landon's car.

"We're almost there. You won't believe the view. It's spectacular."

Emma wanted to check her phone to make sure she still had service and to see if there was any update from Landon—sometimes he had Internet access on his flights—but Margaret had made it clear in the past that she felt cell phones were rude and intrusive. She especially didn't like it when Emma used her phone while driving; once again, it wasn't worth the fuss Margaret made.

The sky was cloudy but not threatening, but the wind had picked up. She thought of Landon, and her worry doubled. She was anxious to get home.

"Anyway, I want to finish this while it's on my mind. Like I said, I am leaving everything to you, dear."

Emma had her foot on the brake to slow the SUV as they went over some bumps and she pushed too hard, throwing them both forward.

"I'm sorry, are you okay?"

Margaret laughed. "Yes, I'm fine."

"Margaret, why would you do—"?

"You are the only one who has earned it. Of course there are a few details and stipulations we will need to go over, but basically it's all going to you."

"I don't know what to say. I mean, thank you, of course, but I'm still stunned by the news."

"I'm sure you are. We can talk more about it after it sinks in. Oh look, there's the rock formation and the lone tree, as Jonathan used to call it. We are close."

They had now left civilization and all communication behind.

Through a small clearing amidst the thick pines, Emma saw a log structure, too nice to be called rustic. "Wow, that's a cabin?"

Tucked away in a grove of towering pine trees, the spacious log home had a wraparound porch, a high-pitched roof, and gabled windows. Two large, picture windows balanced the front of the cabin, and a large porch swing sat invitingly near the front door.

"It's wonderful, isn't it?"

Emma nodded. She could see why Margaret longed to visit the cabin. Certainly their family had shared some special memories there. The place looked like it had all the luxuries of home but provided an outdoorsy atmosphere. It was rustically elegant.

"I'm so glad you like it. I knew you would, once you were here."

Margaret suggested they park around back, so Emma steered the car to the backside of the structure and slowed to a stop.

For a cabin that had sat vacant for so many years, it looked well cared for and in good repair. Of course it was possible that they had a hired hand to look over the place.

She allowed herself a moment to think about Margaret's revelation about her inheriting the family fortune. Material things really weren't a huge focus in her life, but the feeling of security was nice. And the fact that this lovely cabin could actually belong to her one day . . . she couldn't even begin to wrap her brain around it.

Fumbling in her purse, Margaret finally found what she was looking for. "I was nervous there for a minute." She pulled out a set of keys.

Emma hurried around to the passenger side and helped Margaret out of the car. The woman refused her wheelchair and allowed Emma to assist her to the cabin door; then Margaret attempted to unlock it. After trying several keys without success, she handed the keys to Emma.

Emma began to worry, having no luck on the first and second try, but on the third, the key slid easily into the lock and the knob turned. They were in.

Once she helped Margaret get settled in a chair, Emma unloaded a few bags from the car then joined her mother-in-law in the living room.

"So, how do you like it?"

Emma turned in a circle, drinking in the beauty of the cabin. High-beamed ceilings and a large fireplace created an open, inviting space. Wooden planked floors and log pole walls made it warm and cozy, but the "cowboy chic" décor kept it elegant. Bronze animal sculptures and paintings of Western landscapes brought the outdoors inside. "It's really lovely, Margaret. Nicer than most homes I've been in."

"I guess it lacks the bear-skin rug and moose motifs most cabins have, but we were accustomed to certain comforts we weren't willing to go without."

"Well, it's beautiful and very comfortable." Emma sat on the soft camel-colored leather couch with brightly colored Native American woven pillows and put her feet up on the ottoman.

"How are you feeling, Margaret? Can I get you anything?"

"Not right now, dear. I'd just like to rest a moment."

"Do you mind if I look around?"

"Not at all. Make yourself at home."

Margaret closed her eyes, and Emma pushed herself to her feet.

The living area boasted a built-in bookcase with a flat screen TV and an expensive stereo system. As she studied the paintings, she recognized several from artists Jonathan had in his own collection. She'd given most of his things to Margaret, unsure of what to do with them.

The kitchen had every possible appliance and up-to-date convenience as well as a large eight-seat, hand-carved dining table. Also on the main floor was a laundry room and pantry. Out of curiosity, Emma opened the pantry doors and found each shelf to be well stocked with canned goods and boxes of pasta and other foods. She went back to the fridge and opened the door. Inside there was a variety of vegetables and lunchmeats, cheeses, and a gallon of fresh milk.

Clearly Margaret had commissioned someone to stock the fridge and pantry, but why in the world did she have so much food on hand?

It didn't make sense for a brief visit.

Emma's stomach clenched at the thought. Something wasn't right.

4

Jess reread Emma's message again then knew what she had to do. Dialing Cassie's number she prepared herself to hear the voice of her high school nemesis, but instead of getting Cassie, she got her voicemail.

"Cassie, this is Emma's friend, Jess. Please call me when you get this message."

Jess hung up the phone and checked to see if there had been a text from Emma in the thirty seconds it had taken to call Cassie.

Nothing.

Pacing the floor of her apartment, Jess couldn't help the concern that was filling her head. Even though Emma had sent a text to cancel their lunch date, she had added the "code" request. Her guess was that Margaret was keeping her occupied and Emma wanted an excuse to get away. But why wasn't she answering her phone?

She'd driven by Emma's house just to see if maybe she was there, but no one was home.

The vibration of the phone in her hand startled her.

"Cassie!" she answered quickly. "Thanks for calling!"

"Sorry I missed you. I was with a client when you called." Cassie's voice was formal.

The last person Jess wanted to have contact with was Cassie, but Cassie was the only other friend of Emma's who she had a number for. If she weren't desperate, she wouldn't be calling. Besides, there was a chance Cassie didn't know that she was the same Jess from high school. Right now none of that mattered. She hoped Cassie had Landon's number; if anyone had heard from Emma, it would be Landon.

"Have you heard from Emma?"

"Hmm, not since this morning. Why?"

"We were supposed to meet for lunch, but she cancelled on me at the last minute. Actually, I'd waited for half an hour before she texted me to cancel."

"What did Emma say?"

"Just that something had come up. I'm just a little worried about her."

"I'm sure she's fine. Maybe she got a call from a client and is in the middle of a photo shoot and can't talk."

"I'm sure you're right and that it's nothing. It's just that she said she'd explain later. She was on her way to see her mother-in-law before we were going for lunch."

"Oh, poor Emma. She doesn't love being with her mother-in-law. That woman could make the Wicked Witch of the East sound like Mother Theresa."

Jess couldn't help but laugh. "I'm just hoping you have Landon's number. I want to contact him and see if he's heard from her. Something just doesn't feel right."

"I have his number right here." She gave her the number of Landon's cell phone. "Would you mind sending me a quick text when you find out what's going on?"

"Not at all."

"I'll put you in my phone so I'll know it's you. You said, Jess, right?"

"Yes." She didn't offer her last name.

"Okay. I'll watch for your text."

Jess ended the call and snickered. Cassie had no idea who she was. Part of her wondered what Cassie's reaction would be when she found out.

She punched Landon's number into her phone and waited for him to pick up. It didn't ring but went straight to his voicemail. It was possible he was still en route to wherever in Europe he was going. She left a voicemail message and tried not to convey the overwhelming concern she felt.

Then she had a thought. She could call the care center and ask to speak with Margaret!

Using her phone to search for the care center, she realized she didn't know the name of the place, but luckily she knew the area. Deducing the coordinates of all the options, she found the center that fit the location Emma had described in a previous conversation.

"Whispering Pines," the woman said.

"Hi, could I please speak with Margaret Lowell, please?"

"Um, may I ask who's calling?"

"Oh, I'm sorry. I'm a friend of Mrs. Lowell's daughter-in-law, and I need to get in touch with her, but she's not answering her phone. The last time I heard from her she was with Mrs. Lowell."

"I see. Well, Mrs. Lowell is no longer a resident at Whispering Pines. In fact, she left with her daughter-in-law today. Her belongings were sent to storage."

"Hmm, well, I guess that's why she's not answering her phone. She's probably busy helping Mrs. Lowell get settled. Okay then, I appreciate your help."

She ended the call and chewed her bottom lip. Is that all it was? She was just helping Margaret get settled in her new place? She had no choice but to be patient and wait for Emma to contact her.

She sent a quick text to Cassie, saying she still hadn't heard from Emma, then decided to run a few errands before the winter storm that was quickly approaching slammed the Pacific Northwest.

* * *

Emma had gone upstairs to see the bedrooms, but something about the growing shadows, increasing wind, and remoteness of the cabin sent chills up her spine. They needed to get on the road. She no longer cared about the fancy cabin or why they'd come; she just wanted to get back to civilization, and she desperately needed to know that Landon was okay.

Descending the stairs, making as much noise as she could to wake Margaret, she steeled herself with courage to tell her mother-in-law that it was time to leave. She didn't want to drive down in the dark ,and by the sound of the wind in the trees, it was possible the storm was coming soon, and at this elevation snow was very possible.

"Oh, good, you're awake," Emma exclaimed when she entered the room.

"I just needed a quick rest. I tire quite easily." She covered her mouth with a handkerchief and coughed into it several times then clutched the hankie to her chest and drew in several breaths.

"Margaret, are you okay?"

"I'm fine, dear. Please don't worry about me."

"Well, then it's probably time for us to head back to town. I noticed it was getting dark fast, and I don't really want to drive down in the dark."

"I understand." Margaret tried to push herself up from the chair but didn't seem to have the strength. "One of the reasons I brought you here was to give you something."

Emma helped her get to her feet, a feeling of urgency tightening her stomach muscles.

Fine, let's just get this over with so we can get out of here.

They walked to the kitchen where Margaret sat in a chair at the dining table and directed Emma to open a cabinet and bring her a medium-sized box.

"One of the things I used to do when we came to the cabin was scrapbook."

Emma had to hold in a burst of laughter. "You scrapbook?"

"I know. I wouldn't believe it if I were you either, but the truth is, I really enjoy it. It's very relaxing and was a great way to spend my days here while Jonathan and his father went fishing or hunting. And that's what I wanted to give you." She tried to open the flaps but just didn't have the strength. "Do you mind, dear?"

Emma pulled the flaps of the box open.

"Go ahead," Margaret said, "take out the binders."

Unloading several binders from the box, Emma opened the cover of the first one and smiled. Looking back at her was a photo of her and Jonathan, on their wedding day.

With the turning of each beautifully decorated page, Emma felt herself slipping back in time. Photos of her and Jonathan together at family gatherings and social functions, pictures of them on vacations and throughout their courtship, were expertly scrapbooked into clever and colorful pages.

Seeing pictures she hadn't seen in years, feeling the emotions the pictures triggered, brought tears to her eyes.

"I can't believe you did this," Emma said, wiping a tear from her eye. In the photos she and Jonathan created an image worthy of a magazine cover. Jonathan was incredibly striking with piercing blue eyes; thick, golden hair; a wide, gorgeous smile; and sun-kissed skin. He'd been approached to model more than once. Emma's coloring matched her husband's, but she had blonde highlights and green eyes. Together they looked like the all-American fairytale couple.

A few months into her marriage, she'd begun to suspect Jonathan was hiding something from her. He spent far too much time at work and spent a great deal of time at his office. She asked him what was going on, but he denied that he was doing anything wrong. He had enough of a temper that she never pressed him, but in her heart she knew there was a problem.

His actions over their two years of marriage were suspicious enough to confirm her fears. He was having affairs and carrying on with women at the hospital, women in their social circle, and even women from the street. It seemed like everyone knew about it, but no one talked about it. Especially to her.

After his death, Emma never felt a need to dig for definitive proof. It didn't matter. He was gone, and she was in enough pain without having to add to it by finding out about his questionable behavior.

"These scrapbooks are really incredible. How long did it take you to make them?"

When Margaret didn't answer her directly, Emma looked over at her. The woman was dabbing her face and neck with her handkerchief. Her cheeks were flushed.

"Margaret, oh my goodness, are you all right?"

"I'm fine dear, just feeling a bit warm."

"Do you need something cold to drink? What can I get you?"

"I could use a glass of water and maybe something to eat. Sometimes this happens when my blood sugar gets low."

"Of course!" Emma jumped to her feet and rushed to the kitchen. She berated herself for allowing Margaret to talk her into coming to the cabin when the woman's health was so poor. Thinking back, she really questioned whether the care center actually knew and approved of her leaving. If something bad happened while they were gone, she would be held responsible.

In the fridge she found cold cuts and cheese and quickly made a sandwich for Margaret. With a plate in one hand and glass of ice water in the other, Emma raced back to her mother-in-law's side.

"Here you go," Emma said, helping her take some sips of water.

Margaret closed her eyes and took some slow, deep breaths.

"How about some of this sandwich?" Emma offered the food, and Margaret took a bite then chewed slowly and swallowed.

"Thank you, dear. I already feel better."

Emma helped her with a few more bites and sips of water till the woman had gotten her fill.

"Margaret, may I ask you something?"

"Of course you can."

"Did the care center actually give their consent for you to leave with me?"

"I told them I was going out with you."

"Out, away from the center, or outside, on the grounds, like we usually do?"

Margaret's expression changed, her forehead wrinkling, her eyelids narrowing, her lips pursing angrily. After a moment, she burst out with, "Those people don't give two hoots about me. They knew I was leaving, but honestly I can't go back! I've had enough of that place!"

Taken aback, Emma tried to process what exactly her mother-in-law was saying. The fridge was filled with food. The cabin had been prepared for their arrival. How long had Margaret really planned on staying?

"I can help you find another center, one you will like better," Emma said.

Margaret didn't answer, the stubborn expression on her face reminding Emma of a pouting child.

Then a thought occurred to her. "Margaret, you weren't thinking of staying here alone, were you?"

Margaret closed her eyes, refusing to answer.

Beside herself with worry, Emma looked out at the darkening sky, concerned about driving back in the dark.

"Margaret, we have to talk about this. It's getting dark, and we need to get on the road. I can't stay the night. I need to check on Landon, my friends will be worried about me, and I've got work to do and deadlines to meet. And I'm sorry, but I won't leave you here."

Pressing her handkerchief to her forehead, Margaret nodded. "All right, I suppose you're right. I just feel so weak. I need a minute while my blood sugar levels out."

"I'll let you rest while I put this away." Emma helped her to a chair in the living room then put things away in the kitchen. She knew Margaret wasn't happy at the rest home, but she didn't think the woman was desperate enough to go to these lengths to get out. Living here alone, especially with winter coming on, wasn't wise at all. As far as she knew, no one knew they were here. If anything happened, no one would know where to find them. Emma's heart began to race.

In the kitchen, she stopped and looked out the window as the final rays of light disappeared. She wanted to kick herself for letting Margaret talk her into this. That woman! Somehow she managed to bully and manipulate people into doing her will. It was time for Emma to stand up to her.

Checking her phone for service for the thousandth time, and finding none, she gave up and headed for the living room. Her reflection in the microwave window caught her eye. She stopped and whispered to herself, "Don't be such a chicken. Go tell her you are leaving right now!"

Pulling back her shoulders, she gave a perfunctory nod of her head, and filled with resolve, she turned and headed out of the room.

When she got to Margaret, the woman was sound asleep, and to Emma's alarm her face was flushed and her forehead damp.

Emma felt her cheek. She didn't feel feverish; in fact, she felt cold.

"Margaret," Emma said, trying not to startle her.

Margaret didn't budge.

"Margaret," Emma said louder, jiggling her mother-in-law's shoulder.

Still there was no response.

"Margaret," Emma cried, shaking her vigorously.

"Emma?" she said weakly.

"Oh!" Emma clapped a hand to her heart. "Margaret, you had me scared there for a second. We have to leave right now. We have to get you back. You aren't well."

"I'm going to be fine, dear. Please don't fuss. I just fell asleep."

"But you're covered in a cold sweat."

"That happens when my blood sugar drops."

"I'm relieved to hear that's all it is, but I still think it's time we left."

"That's fine, but please, I need to rest a little longer," Margaret said. "I'm just so weak."

Emma closed her eyes and drew in a calming breath. It didn't work.

"Please, dear. You need to calm down and relax. Let me rest a bit, and we can leave after that."

Typical of Margaret, the discussion was over. It was her way or no way.

Emma looked at the feeble woman in the chair and wondered how someone who looked so harmless could still be so controlling.

Fine! She would let the woman rest, but she didn't care if it was 3:00 in the morning, they were getting off that mountain tonight!

With nothing to do she found a book that looked interesting and turned on the lamp next to the sofa.

She barely got the first page read before the long day caught up with her. Before she could start the next page, she too was asleep.

5

THE SCRAPING OF BRANCHES AND howling of wind woke her with a start. Emma jumped to her feet, and the book on her lap crashed to the floor.

She raced to the window and let out a cry when she looked outside. All she could see was a swirl of white. It was impossible to know how long it had been snowing, but she knew there was no way they could get down the mountain tonight. It was as if Margaret controlled the weather too!

The lamp shed light across the room to Margaret who was slumped in her chair. She looked horribly uncomfortable, and Emma didn't have the heart to leave her there.

Doubting she could get the woman upstairs to the bedroom, she opted for the sofa and managed to get Margaret awake enough to get her to move across the room and lie down.

Covering her with an afghan, she tucked her in then headed for the chair where Margaret had been sleeping. She found another afghan and settled in for a long night.

"Thank you, dear," Margaret said. "It feels good to have someone who loves me taking care of me."

Emma didn't know what to say. She felt totally taken advantage of, yet she felt sorry for the woman.

The howling wind rattled the windows, trying to get inside where it was warm. Emma felt churned up inside and angry with herself for being such an easy target for Margaret. She needed to stand up for herself.

The worst part of it all was that she had no idea how Landon was. In the dark, unfamiliar surroundings, her worst fears surfaced. She couldn't shut her eyes because she saw images of plane crashes and bodies everywhere. She prayed for his safety and for the night to pass quickly. As soon as it was light, they were leaving.

* * *

The first thing Emma did when she woke up was check her phone for service.

"Dear, the only place we get cell service is up on the ridge to the East. I'm sorry. I'm sure your fiancé is as worried about you as you are about him."

He would be trying to contact her to let her know he landed safely. What was he thinking when she wasn't answering his calls or texts?

"I'm sure you're right," Emma said, looking across the room at Margaret, who seemed awfully perky at the moment.

"You're probably ready to head out as soon as we can."

"Yes. I'm anxious to find out how he is, and I have a lot of work to finish. I have some appointments I can't miss today." She was hoping to go house hunting with Cassie.

"Good thing we have your fiancé's four-wheel drive. We're going to need it."

Emma wondered just how many inches they'd gotten. She opened the front door open to look out and nearly burst into tears. The snow was up to the second step and still coming down.

Anger began to boil inside her, the surge of emotion causing her to tremble. Clenching her fists, she turned to Margaret.

"You knew it was going to snow, didn't you?" She kept her voice steady, but there was steam behind her words.

"I knew there was a storm coming, but I had no idea it would snow this much." Margaret folded her arms across her chest and looked at Emma with piercing eyes. " What are you trying to say?"

"I don't know what I'm trying to say," Emma blurted out. "I just know that for some reason you wanted to delay our leaving. I understand you don't want to go back to the care center, and I promise we can find you a better place to live. I won't leave you here alone, but I need to get home."

"All right, I'm ready when you are."

Emma pulled on her coat and braced herself for the walk to the car. She didn't care what it took; she was getting them out of there, now!

"Do you have a snow shovel?" she asked.

"There is a closet near the back door. There should be a shovel in there."

Emma stormed through the house. The anger inside of her would help her plow through the cold and the snow. Nothing would stop her from getting off that mountain.

Finding the shovel, she stomped out the back door, stepping onto the snow-laden porch. Her feet flew out from under her, and she landed on her side with a thud.

The pain in her hip and ribs took her breath, and she couldn't move for several moments. Once her breathing returned, she slowly straightened, wincing at the stabbing pain in her ribs. Pushing herelf up she finally got to her feet and stood for a minute to get her bearings. Anger quickly kicked back in, and she took the shovel and stabbed it into the thick blanket of snow. Crying out in pain as she lifted the heavy shovelful of snow, she forged ahead, ignoring the icy bite on her feet as her short boots quickly became filled with snow.

Slipping again on the slick surface of the porch but keeping her balance, she braced herself as she shoveled a narrow path to the car, which luckily was close to the back door. The falling snow covered her hair, shoulders, and back, and her uncovered hands had gone numb, but adrenalin kept her going.

Finally, she managed to get the snow cleared so they could get to the vehicle. She didn't allow herself to worry about how dangerous the drive down the mountain would be. It was a risk she was willing to take.

Throwing the shovel against the porch railing, she clamored into the house, bringing a layer of snow with her.

"Margaret," she called, looking around the room, "I'm done. We can leave."

"Just a minute, dear." The woman was in the kitchen.

Emma shook her head to get the flakes out of her hair and took off her coat and shook it. She needed to get a towel to wipe up the puddles of melting snow.

Walking into the kitchen, she startled Margaret, who spun around from the counter wielding a giant butcher knife.

Emma gasped.

"Sorry, dear." Margaret put down the knife. "I thought I'd throw together a few sandwiches since we aren't eating breakfast, and it may take a while to drive down in this weather."

"I think we'd better get going. It's going to get worse before it gets better."

"I'll just put these in a bag, and we can leave."

Emma pulled several paper towels off the roll and squeezed some of the moisture from her wet hair. She then wiped up the puddles on the hardwood floor.

Margaret appeared holding a bag and her coat. "I'm ready."

Turning out lights and turning off the furnace, Margaret took one last look around. "Oh, don't forget the scrapbooks. You can put them in this to protect them." She handed Emma the plastic grocery bag.

At the moment Emma didn't care about them, but she wanted to remain as civil as possible, especially since at any moment she was about the crack.

Grabbing the stack of books, Emma slid them into a grocery bag. Margaret locked the door, and they pulled it behind them as they left.

"Here," Margaret said, handing her the keys. "It's yours now."

Emma didn't want the cabin; she also didn't want to add drama to the situation. They could work it out later. Right now they needed to get on the road.

Helping Margaret get inside the SUV, Emma tromped around to the other side and climbed in behind the steering wheel. Already she felt better. Just sitting inside Landon's truck and knowing she was only a few hours from home gave her renewed energy and strength. She plugged her phone into the charger since it was almost dead.

Saying a quick prayer in her mind, she started the engine and turned on the heater. She was wet and cold and needed to quit shivering so she could concentrate.

Hoping the all-wheel-drive vehicle would handle the conditions, she put the car in reverse so she could turn the SUV around then gave it some gas.

Moving slowly the SUV crept back a few inches then the wheels lost traction. She put the car in drive and went forward until the wheels spun in place. Back and forth they rocked as she attempted to turn the car around so they could travel down the snowy road. They made slow progress, but it was progress nonetheless and she wasn't giving up.

Finally, getting the car turned around, she steered it toward the road and met up with resistance again. Spinning wheels and the deep snow made movement in any direction a challenge. Going back and forth again helped her create a length of packed snow to get a running start. She figured if she backed up and then really gunned the engine she would get enough momentum to propel the vehicle through the snow then the downhill slope of the road would keep them going.

Backing up until the bank of snow stopped her, she took a deep breath, told Margaret to hold on, and then stomped on the gas.

The SUV picked up speed and barreled into the untouched snow. Just as Emma predicted, the speed and force helped them onto the road and kept them going, but she quickly realized she had absolutely no control. As soon as the road began to bend to the left, she knew they were in big trouble. The road turned, but the slick snow prevented the wheels of the car from following. The SUV turned just enough to slide sideways off the road then slammed up against a large pine tree, the impact shaking an avalanche of snow onto the SUV.

Silence settled in on them, except for the wet splattering of heavy snowflakes falling.

Her mind raced, her chest filled with panic. How were they going to get off that mountain?

"I'm so sorry, Margaret, are you okay?" She turned and saw the woman lying still with her head against the window.

"Margaret!" She shook Margaret's shoulder. "Are you okay?"

Margaret groaned and immediately put her hand to her head. "What happened?"

"We slid off the road. Are you okay?"

"I think so." She looked at her hand. "No blood."

"I'm so sorry. I don't know what we're going to do now." Emma couldn't hold back the tears. Her emotions were heightened by the crash, and she was at her wits' end.

"It's going to be all right," Margaret assured her. "The ranger will come and check on us and help us out. I bet we see him as soon as the snow stops. Don't worry, dear. It's going to be fine."

"I guess there's nothing to do but go back to the cabin. Can you make it?"

"I'll be fine. I'm tougher than you think," Margaret replied.

It took some doing to get out. Because the snow was so deep, it was difficult to open the doors. With some effort she finally got hers to open and helped Margaret climb over the console and out the driver's side.

They were about to head for the cabin when Emma remembered her phone. She removed the phone from the charger and noticed she had one bar of service.

Excitement shot through her like a charge from a light socket. She dialed 911.

The phone rang. Her heart skipped several beats. They were saved!

A voice on the other end answered, but the voice stopped and the line went dead before either of them said anything.

"Hello! Hello!" She looked at the phone and could see that the call was still connected. Maybe they could hear her. "Please help us. We are stranded at the Charles Lowell cabin somewhere up Whistler's Canyon area." She looked at the phone, but the call had stopped. The bar was gone. She maneuvered her phone around to see if she could pick up another signal. But there was nothing.

"Emma, dear. Did you reach help?" Margaret asked.

"For just a moment, but the call got dropped," she said as tears threatened.

She hesitated to leave the area, in case she got service, but the two women were chilled to the bone, so they trudged back to the cabin. They were almost to the front steps when Emma realized that in all of the excitement of having phone service for a few moments she'd forgotten the car keys in the ignition. She was too cold to go back and get them. She would find some warmer clothes and go out later. Right now she needed to get inside. She'd never been so cold in her life.

Using the key Margaret had given her, Emma opened the front door, and they both hurried inside.

"I'll make us something warm to drink," Margaret said.

"Are you sure you don't want me to do it? How is your head?"

"I got a bit of a goose-egg, but I'm fine. There are some dry clothes in the spare bedroom upstairs. Why don't you change before you catch cold? I'll turn on the heat, and we can light the gas log and get things warmed up in here."

Emma appreciated Margaret's concern and climbed the stairs to find the bedroom where the clothes were.

Just as Margaret said, the closet had several western, snap-front shirts and jeans hanging, as well as a man's tracksuit. Opting for the comfort of the tracksuit, Emma pulled off her heavy, wet jeans and slid on the warm, loose track pants. She scoured the drawers and found several pair of socks and underclothes items. The warmth of dry socks immediately took the chill off, and she began to feel warmth return to her feet.

A knock at the door sounded.

"Come in."

Margaret walked inside, carrying a tray with two steaming mugs. "Oh, good. I see you had some luck. I bet that feels better."

"Much. Thank you."

"This will help. I didn't have any marshmallows though."

Margaret handed her a mug of cocoa.

"Mmm, it smells heavenly. Thank you."

Emma sat on the bed, and Margaret took her own mug and sat in the chair in the corner.

"I'm sorry about what just happened," Emma said. "I think I panicked."

"That's okay, dear. No harm done. Help will come. I feel badly that this has caused you trouble with your schedule."

"I'm hoping that some of my texts went through when we had service. I texted my fiancé and I texted my realtor friend to let her know I wouldn't make our appointment."

Margaret stopped drinking. "Did they go through?"

"It seemed that way, but I can't tell. My phone died." Emma noticed that Margaret seemed concerned. "If they did go through, maybe they'll think to send help."

"Did you tell them where you were?" Margaret pressed.

"I tried to. I'm not exactly sure where we are."

Margaret smiled. "Like my husband used to say, we're in the middle of nowhere."

"That's certainly how it feels."

"Well, we're safe and warm for the time being. Thank goodness we have food to keep us for as long as we need to be here."

"I was wondering about that." Emma began to feel warm and fuzzy inside. "Why . . . is there"—she stopped to yawn—"so much food? Were you really planning on leaving the assisted living center and staying here for good?"

Her vision began to blur. She blinked several times, but it didn't help.

"Actually, yes. I wasn't planning on going back."

"But you can't stay"—she yawned again her body feeling like it was starting to melt—"alone."

Margaret got up and took the mug of cocoa from her.

"I don't plan on being alone," she said.

"Oh?" The room began to spin. "What do you mean?" Her words slurred together, her arms growing limp, her head feeling heavy.

"You're staying with me."

* * *

Nightmares of sliding in the snow; of Landon coming to help her, reaching for her but their hands not meeting; and of her sitting at the bottom of a hole in the ground and dirt being shoveled on her, burying her alive, plagued her as she slept.

Where was she? Why was she there? What was happening to her?

She felt as if she knew something was wrong but had no idea what it was or how to fix it.

Help! The words formed in her mind, but she didn't know if she said them out loud or not. Was she dreaming that she was dreaming? Or was something happening that only seemed like it was a dream?

Whatever it was, she couldn't break the hold it had on her, and slowly, just as she was about to touch the surface of reality, she slipped down into the dark unknown.

6

EARLY THE NEXT MORNING, JESS answered a phone call as she slowed her pace on the treadmill. Jogging indoors was not her favorite, but the drizzle outside was too heavy for an outdoor run.

"Jess, it's Landon."

"Hi, Landon." She straddled the slowing treadmill and took several breaths. "How are—"

"Where's Emma?" he exclaimed. "Did you find her?"

"No. Haven't you heard from her?"

"She hasn't answered my calls or my texts. What's going on? Where is she?"

"I was hoping you could tell me. I knew if anyone had heard from her it would be you. Landon, I've been by her house, I've called and texted her a dozen times, I even called out to her mother-in-law's care center."

"What did you find out?"

"Nothing. The person at the care center said Emma had been there but that she left with Margaret earlier that day."

"Emma said she was going over to visit her."

"Right, that's why she cancelled lunch with me. The strange thing is, they told me that Margaret had checked out of the care center for good. They were sending her belongings to a storage facility."

"Hmm, that doesn't really make sense. According to Margaret that was the best and only facility she would even consider moving too. Emma didn't say anything about her moving to another place."

"Yeah, I was surprised—"

"I take that back," he said quickly. "It sounds exactly like her. She's the type of woman who is never happy. Never satisfied."

"She sounds like the mother-in-law from your worst nightmare," Jess said.

"Emma has tried to help her and be there when she needs her, but her demands are unreasonable most of the time. I wonder what she's up to. Somehow she's got Emma involved, and most likely Emma isn't happy about it."

"She didn't even want to go see her yesterday, and when she cancelled lunch with me, she told me to send her the code in four hours."

"The code?"

"Yeah, we came up with a system whenever we needed help getting out of a situation. We text the other person and tell them to either call or send a message that there is an emergency or an appointment we've forgotten, giving us an excuse to leave. So the fact that she hasn't come home seems a little bizarre, don't you think?" Jess asked.

"You don't think she's even been home?"

"It doesn't seem like it. I looked inside her mailbox, and she hasn't even picked up her mail."

"Now that's totally not like Emma. Ever since she had a check stolen out of her mailbox, she's a fanatic about getting her mail every day."

"I know! I've picked it up for her several times when she's had to work late. She doesn't like leaving it in the box. I can't help but think . . ."

She didn't want to say what she was thinking.

"What, Jess?"

"I know this sounds terrible, but Margaret seems like she's manipulative enough and controlling enough she's probably forcing Emma to help her find a new place to live. But why can't she call and let us know? That's the part that just doesn't make sense."

"Emma's too nice to say anything bad about anyone, so when she tells me that Margaret is being unreasonable or demanding, I believe her," Landon said.

"I think that woman is up to something," Jess said. "Emma's told me too many bizarre things about Margaret. The woman sounds like she's capable of anything!"

"You're scaring me," Landon said.

"I'm scaring myself. I just don't know what to do to get in touch with Emma."

"I hate this! I'm halfway around the world and can't do a thing!"

"Listen," Jess said, deciding she needed to be reasonable and not jump to conclusions. "I'm sure there's a good explanation. She may be somewhere without cell service, or her phone is dead and she doesn't have a charger with her. I bet we hear from her any minute now."

"I hope you're right, Jess, or I'm getting on the next plane home. I can't stand the thought of something happening to her."

"I have a friend who works at the police department. I could call him and ask him for help."

"That would be great, Jess. Would you mind doing that? Oops, hold on for one second. I've got to take this call."

Jess held the line and waited for Landon to come back on. She reviewed the events in her head and fought the urge to panic. Something was definitely wrong.

"Jess?" Landon came back on. "Will you do me a favor?"

"Sure, anything."

"Will you go by her house again? See if you can see anything then call me. I have a few things on this end I can do in the meantime."

"I'll leave right now."

* * *

Blinding sunlight hit Emma's face. She held her hand up to shield her eyes, which she opened to a slit then quickly shut again. Her head pounded, a thick, heavy throbbing that felt like it was going to shatter her skull.

As her consciousness surfaced, she became more aware of her discomfort. Her neck and spine ached, and a stomach-curdling wave of nausea washed over her. She moved her arm to grab her abdomen, but the muscle in her shoulder seized up with a hot, gripping pain.

What was going on? Had she caught some horrible virus?

"Good morning."

Emma jumped and cried out in pain. She pulled in several breaths to calm her stomach, threatening to empty its contents.

After a moment, she opened her eyes to see Margaret standing next to the bed.

"Hello, Emma."

Emma swallowed, closing her eyes again. "You scared the life out of me!"

"Well, you scared the life out of me yesterday when you nearly killed me in that crash," Margaret responded. Her tone was forceful and exact. She sounded nothing like the pathetic, sickly old woman of the past two days.

"Margaret, I'm sorry." She forced herself to look at the woman. "I didn't mean for that to happen. I should have been patient and waited for help."

Margaret laughed.

"What?"

"That's never been one of your best virtues, has it? Being impatient and demanding to my son didn't help him love you any more, did it?"

The old Margaret had returned.

"I don't understand," Emma said, the feeling of sickness not subsiding. It was all she could do to get the words out. "What do you mean?"

"He was a devoted husband and provider, he did everything you ever asked of him, yet it never was enough. You wanted a bigger house? He gave you a bigger house. You wanted a new car? He gave you a new car. But you weren't satisfied."

"That's not true!" She tried to sit up, but she felt completely drained of strength. What was going on? "I never asked for those things," she whispered.

"He bent over backwards to please you. Yet you weren't there for him. You were never much of a wife to him when he was alive. You couldn't even provide a child, which he desperately wanted."

Knowing that arguing back would only throw fuel onto the flame, Emma breathed steadily, trying to remain calm. "Margaret, those things you accuse me of are not true. Jonathan was the one who wanted a bigger house and a new car. I swear. And he was the one who wanted to wait to have children. Every month I begged him to try visiting a fertility specialist, but he always said he wasn't really ready to start a family anyway."

"That's not what he told me, Emma. He used to come to me so upset that your marriage wasn't what he expected it would be. Of course, I told him countless time to divorce you, but he didn't want to put our family name and his reputation through that."

She moved her arm again and couldn't contain the whimper of pain she released. Something was seriously wrong. "None of this is true," she said breathlessly. Luckily the nausea was subsiding. She'd never told her mother-in-law the truth about her son because now that Jonathan was gone she thought it didn't matter. But maybe it did. Emma wasn't going to take this kind of garbage from her, especially when she didn't deserve it.

"You were never good enough for my son! I knew it from the moment I met you. I knew he would be unhappy if he married you, and he was."

"Margaret, please try and understand this." Emma exercised every ounce of self-control she had. "I did everything I could to make your son happy. I loved him, I wanted our marriage to work, but . . ."

Margaret looked at her with daring in her eyes, still convinced her son was a saint.

Before she could stop herself, Emma burst out with, "He was unfaithful to me from the day we were married!"

Margaret's eyes widened, her mouthed dropped open, then her expression changed to anger, and she slapped Emma hard across the face.

The crack in her jaw and painful sting across her cheek took her breath. She held the side of her head with her hand.

"How dare you speak ill of my son! I won't have it. Whatever he did, I'm sure he had his reasons and that you deserved it!"

Even though Emma exercised a huge amount of restraint to hold her tongue, she couldn't stop the tears that spilled onto her cheeks. It didn't matter what she said, there was nothing she could do to prove to his mother that her son had been a horrible, unfaithful husband.

"Men of Jonathan's status are different from most men, and you never understood the social obligation of being his wife. There are different rules with men like him. I'm sure you felt you were having to sacrifice certain things and look the other way, but the great honor and prestige of being his wife was well worth it."

Emma's sick and weakened state helped her hide the shock and disgust she felt at Margaret's revelation. There was nothing that excused his treatment of her and his complete disregard for the sanctity of their marriage.

"I never understood what he saw in you and how you never really caught on to the privileged lifestyle that marriage to my son afforded you. It certainly caused me plenty of grief; however, there is one way you can redeem yourself. You weren't worthy of him when he was alive, but you can prove yourself worthy of him now."

Emma felt anger and outrage ignite in her chest, her heightened emotions constricting her throat. No matter how ridiculous Margaret's views were and how wrong they were, Emma had to take into account that Margaret had snapped, and she didn't dare aggravate her further. Who knew what the woman was capable of?

"I will help you become pure and worthy of his love. You owe that to him, and you owe it to me!"

Emma had no idea what the woman was talking about. She'd been nothing but devoted and faithful to Jonathan, but Margaret seemed too incensed and convinced to talk rationally. Her instincts told her to stay quiet, which meant not pointing out that Margaret's own husband had been a philanderer and a womanizer. Of course, Margaret most likely understood all of that.

Emma feared the wild-eyed madness in Margaret's expression. The woman had completely lost touch with reality, and Emma didn't doubt for a second that her trip to the cabin had been a smokescreen for deeper motives.

And what exactly did Margaret mean she said she wanted to make Emma pure again?

The thought sent a shiver down her spine.

"If you loved my son as you say you did, then you will soon see the wisdom in what I am doing. You will join me in my vigil."

What in the world was this woman talking about?

"You do as I say and you will have freedom, but if I can't trust you, you won't."

Emma nodded. Staying quiet seemed to be the best way to handle the situation.

She handed Emma the Bible. "Begin by reading the marked passages. We will discuss them at length later. As you fast you will be open to the messages and to the greater purpose our lives have. It wasn't my choice that Jonathan married you, but as you purify yourself, I will learn to accept you."

She pointed to a water bottle on the nightstand. "I will allow you one bottle of water each day. It will sustain you through the process. You will remain in this room until I let you leave. The only water in this room is in the toilet in your bathroom, not in the sink and shower. I wouldn't drink the water in the toilet if you get thirsty, the blue coloring is filled with harmful chemicals."

Emma's mind whirled. She wanted to demand answers, but she was too weak to stand up to Margaret. And in her heart she knew she needed to remain silent.

"I've removed all of your outward worldy attachments and representations. Once you have submitted and proven yourself, I will return your clothing."

Unaware that she wasn't in the tracksuit, she looked down to see she was wearing a long white gown of cotton, plain and simple.

"I needed to prepare you so you would have a complete purification and change of heart. You needed to be stripped of all worldliness."

Horror struck as Emma noticed her engagement ring was missing.

"The ring is safe. Even though you won't be needing it, I saved it with your clothing."

Another wave of shivers crawled up her spine to think Margaret had changed her clothing without her knowledge. What kind of medication had Margaret given her? She also realized the woman was much stronger than she had given her credit for. Especially since she was getting around without her wheelchair.

It had all been an act.

How long had the woman been planning this?

The fear and questions continued to build, and something told her she was now one of those stories from the evening news where people snapped and did crazy, horrible, or heinous things.

"One more thing, you know how I told you a ranger would be coming by to check on us?"

Emma dipped her chin once.

"I lied. We won't see anyone for a month."

Emma couldn't control her reaction. She knew her expression gave away her fears.

"Yes, my darling daughter-in-law, just you and I, together." The satisfaction on her face and in her voice struck terror in Emma's heart. Her flight or fight instinct kicked in, but she held it in. Whatever twisted, illogical thoughts Margaret was having would only be fueled by Emma's reaction.

"Well," she smiled with satisfaction, "I've got soup on the stove. I'll give you a chance to process all of this then I'll be back to check on you."

She got up to leave. Then she stopped. "Trust me, my dear. You don't understand now, but you will thank me for this later."

Without strain or extra effort, she stood and walked out of the room then closed the door. If that wasn't enough, Emma noticed the doorknob had been installed backwards, with the lock on the outside, keeping whoever was inside the room a prisoner. Margaret pushed the button lock, the tiny click confining her to her prison.

Shock set in. What was going on?

Pieces of what Margaret said began to sink in. Fasting. Purification. Being there till spring.

She began to tremble. Another wave of nausea along with panic filled her stomach. She pulled her knees to her chest, wrapped her good arm around her knees, and began to sob. Not wanting Margaret to hear her, she grabbed a pillow and covered her face with it.

Margaret was holding her captive. She was going to cleanse Emma so she would be pure. She was going to starve her. She was going to try to brainwash her.

Why? It had something to do with Jonathan, something to do with Margaret. The woman's twisted brain and unstable emotions and mental condition made Emma think there was plenty to be concerned about. The woman meant business and was apparently willing to do whatever it took to make it happen.

She shut her eyes tightly and began to pray, begging for God to send help, or to help her figure out a way to escape.

She also prayed that God would comfort her and strengthen her. She knew she wasn't alone and that He would hear her prayers.

Rocking back and forth, trying to organize her thoughts and the information she had on the situation just made her panic escalate.

"I can't believe this," she whispered through her tears.

She felt as though she'd lost her grasp on reality. She had to get a grip. She had to keep her wits about her.

But first she had to go to the bathroom.

The wood floor was cold and hard on her feet. The aching, which was now in all of her joints, made walking painful. Somewhere in the last few days she must have picked up a flu bug. That was the only thing that could explain her condition.

Hugging herself with the arm that didn't hurt, she felt the thin cotton gown, which lent no warmth to her slender frame. Just as Margaret had said, the water in the toilet was blue. Ice blue, like Margaret's heart.

Even though Margaret had told her there was no water in the sink, she still turned on the faucet. Nothing came out.

There was a pump bottle of hand sanitizer on the counter. She squirted some in her hand and rubbed it into her skin.

Then she looked in the mirror and screamed.

* * *

Jess pulled her car into Emma's driveway then came to a complete stop just behind Emma's car. It was still in the same place as yesterday. Nothing was different. Just one glance told her that Emma still wasn't home.

Her stomach clenched with worry, and again she forced panic from her mind. There had to be a perfectly good explanation for what was going on, she just didn't know what it possibly could be.

With a sigh of frustration, she opened her car door and stepped one foot on the ground then gasped with surprise.

"Sorry," Cassie exclaimed. "I didn't mean to sneak up on you."

With a hand on her heart, Jess, drew in several breaths before she spoke. "I didn't see you."

"I could tell. Hi, I'm Cassie—"

Jess looked at her, waiting for the realization to kick in.

Cassie's gaze narrowed as she studied Jess's face, then her expression melted and her mouth dropped open. "Jess?"

Jess nodded.

"Wow, it's been—"

"Ten years."

Cassie nodded slowly. "How are you?"

"Great," Jess said with a nod. "Just great. You?"

"I'm good, thanks." She glanced at the house then back at Jess. "So, you're friends with Emma?"

"Yep. And you're—"

"Her realtor."

"I know. She gave me your number. I was going to refer a friend to you."

"How nice of you."

Jess didn't tell her she'd changed her mind.

"I hadn't heard back from you, so I thought I would come and check on her. Usually she responds to her messages and texts. It's just . . ."

"Not like her?"

Cassie nodded.

"I talked to Landon, and he asked me to come and check to see if she'd gotten home yet." She walked to the mailbox and opened it.

Her heart dropped. There was even a bigger stack of letters and a magazine inside.

"Is it empty?"

Jess pulled out the pile of mail.

The two women's eyes met.

"Get in!" Cassie said, yanking the car door open. "We can't waste any more time. Something is wrong, and we need to find her!"

Jess wasn't sure she wanted to go anywhere with this woman. She'd caused her the greatest pain she'd had in her life. She was her mortal enemy. Her nemesis. Her—

"Hurry!" Cassie commanded, throwing the passenger side door open.

With her arms full of mail, Jess climbed inside, throwing the letters and magazine onto the back seat. Right now finding Emma was all that mattered.

"We need to create a timeline of events leading up to this moment and see if we can construct some sort of idea of where she could be or at least, where we should start looking," Cassie said.

"I have a notebook in my purse. I can write it all down."

"Good." Cassie backed out of the driveway and pulled onto the road.

"Where are we going?"

"That care center where her mother-in-law lives."

"Her mother-in-law isn't there. I called. They told me she checked out and isn't coming back."

Cassie stopped the car and looked at her. "I don't trust that woman. She's up to something."

"Me neither."

"This isn't good. Something isn't right."

"You're scaring me."

"I'm scaring myself. Buckle up!"

* * *

Emma's reflection in the mirror terrified her. Looking back at her was a gaunt, pale-faced woman with short hair that looked like it had been chopped with hedge clippers.

"My hair!" She pulled at the spiky tufts left from the heinous haircut and began to cry. "Look what she did to my hair!" Thoughts of her wedding and Landon's face when he saw her turned her tears into sobs of frustration and anger.

"How dare she!" She slapped the counter then buried her face in her hands. After a few minutes, her fingers curled and her trembling hands turned into tightly bunched fists.

That was it! She'd had enough. This woman was a fruitcake, and Emma wasn't about to play her stupid game. She'd walk back to Seattle barefoot if she had to before staying here with Margaret for a day, let alone a month.

She rushed to the door and began pounding on it. The more she pounded, the angrier she got. She was younger and stronger than Margaret. She could take this woman. This madness was over!

When she couldn't go on, she felt her hair and got mad again and began pounding louder. How dare that woman do this to her! She was done with this family. All of this talk about Jonathan was garbage. She focused her anger on him. All the lies he told his mother were coming back to haunt her. He'd been unfaithful because he was an egotistical jerk, not because she'd done anything wrong.

She pounded until she dripped with sweat and her knuckles were bruised. She didn't care how mad Margaret got; she would never let that woman control her again.

"Emma, stop that this instant!" Margaret called through the door.

"How could you, Margaret? How could you chop off my hair like that?" Emma's anger and tears fueled her adrenalin, and she banged on the door with renewed strength. "Let me out of here, right now! You can't treat me like this."

"When you calm down, I will open the door," Margaret's placating voice came.

Emma laughed. "Calm down? You're holding me prisoner here for a crime I didn't commit! And you want me to calm down!" She laughed again, feeling she was on the verge of hysteria.

"Calm down, and we can talk about this."

Emma knew that she had to keep her wits about her. It would be the only way to survive this. She turned and fell back against the door holding her head with her hands as sobs of anger, frustration, and confusion tore from her throat. Her intake of breath came in jagged gulps. She held her stomach, clenched with anguish and hunger pains.

"Emma, go back to the bed so I can open the door. This outburst tells me you are ready for the next step."

What step? Emma thought. *What in the world psychotic step is she talking about?* Was there a booklet that told kidnappers and insane people how to hold someone hostage, how to brainwash them, how to torture them?

The only step Emma was taking was one out the door. Landon was probably beside himself with worry. Cassie had probably gone by her house looking for her. Jess was probably wondering where she was. Hopefully someone had notified the authorities that she was missing. Maybe someone at the care center reported Margaret missing and the police were out looking for them. She had to hope this was the case. She had to hope and not factor in the ten inches of snow outside.

A sense of control returned, and Emma wiped her face on the sleeve of her gown as she walked back to the bed.

"Are you on the bed?" Margaret called through the door.

"Yes," Emma said, sitting down on the cheerful floral comforter that belied the asylum she was in.

Margaret unlocked the door and opened it a slit to check that Emma was where she said she would be. Satisfied Emma had obeyed, she opened the door farther. She held up a can of pepper spray.

"Just in case you try to resist me," Margaret explained. She walked into the room. "I need you to understand, I am doing this for the greater good. Just like God expects His people to be worthy before He blesses them, you need to be worthy of the great blessings I am giving you."

Emma nearly burst out laughing. What was she even talking about? Emma eyed the can. She knew she was strong and faster than Margaret. She was willing to take a chance of getting sprayed.

"Resist you?" She lowered her glare. Her muscles tightened as she anticipated her next move. She lowered her chin, hoping to divert Margaret's expectation of her. "Why would I want to—"?

With surprising strength she leapt off the bed prepared to tackle the woman if she had to.

Pffft!

The spray felt like liquid fire on her skin, like a solar flash had suddenly given her the worst sunburn she could imagine. She screamed in pain, the burning in her eyes so bad it was like someone was pulling her eyelids over her head and poking her in the eye with hot coals. The smell assaulted her nostrils and throat causing her to cough and choke.

But that wasn't all; a sudden stabbing volt of pain in her other shoulder brought another cry of pain.

"What . . . ," she coughed, "are you doing to me?" It felt like liquid fire was being shot into the muscle. She barely got the words out and couldn't see anything but began swatting at Margaret with her hands.

"You need to calm down."

Margaret grabbed her arms and forced Emma back to the bed, but Emma continued to resist, though her strength was weakening almost like an energy plug had been pulled and strength was slowly leaking from her.

"You can't do this," Emma cried. "You can't," she coughed, tears streaming down her burning flesh, "just hold someone hostage like this." She struggled, but her arms and fingers relaxed, the muscles losing their strength. "What did you give me?"

"You will eventually understand why I'm doing this, and once you do, you will go along willingly. I just have to keep you here long enough for you to understand my reasons for doing what I'm doing. And until I know you won't hurt yourself, or me, I will keep medicating you. Just trust me, Emma."

The comment struck her funny. Trust her? Was she kidding?

Emma began to laugh, her laughter growing into hysterics, causing her to cough violently, then slowly her coughing stopped and she got weaker and weaker, until she began to drift from consciousness.

"I . . . will . . . never . . . trust . . ." Her words slurred, then she fell into blackness.

7

"WHO'S IN CHARGE HERE?" CASSIE asked the receptionist after she and Jess burst through the front doors.

"I'm sorry, Mrs. Kozlowski isn't available." The receptionist spoke matter-of-factly, raising her chin and giving Cassie a challenging stare.

"Listen," Cassie read the girl's nametag, "Melissa. This is an emergency, and we need to speak to the director of this place. Could you please," she paused and gave her tone a dose of sweetness, "ask Mrs. Kozlowski if she could give us just a moment of her time?"

"It really is urgent," Jess added. She could tell Cassie wasn't going to be denied answers, but she also didn't think this "storm the castle" approach was necessary.

Melissa blew out a breath, looked back and forth at both of the women standing in front of her then said, "Wait here!"

"I'm ready to rip this place apart!" Cassie told Jess. "They have to know something that will help us."

Before Jess could answer, Melissa walked back to her desk.

"Mrs. Kozlowski is in a meeting and can't be disturbed. If you'll leave a number, she will call as soon as she can."

"I'm sorry. Maybe you didn't hear me. This is an emergency. One of your residents, Margaret Lowell's"—Melissa's eyes grew large at the mention of Margaret's name—"daughter-in-law, Emma Lowell, has turned up missing. The last time anyone had any contact with her was before she came here, to visit her mother-in-law."

"Missing?"

"Yes, as in, no contact, no known whereabouts, and no idea where she could possibly be! We need to talk to someone who can help us find out where that crazy woman, Margaret Lowell, could have taken her."

"Wait here," Melissa said, backing away from her desk quickly and knocking her chair over.

Jess noticed the immediate change in Melissa's tone and demeanor at the mention of Margaret's name.

"Now we're getting somewhere," Cassie said.

"No question we came to the right place." Jess's phone buzzed. She'd received a text from her friend Scott who was on the Seattle police force.

In Mexico, on vacation for a week. What do you need?

"Great," she muttered.

"What's wrong?"

"My friend at the police department is out of the country."

"Good morning, ladies," a heavy set woman with a short blonde bob and narrow framed glasses said, as she joined them at the receptionist's desk. "Or is it afternoon?" She checked her watch. "Almost. Goodness, where has this morning gone? I'm Sonja Kozlowski. How can I help you?"

Before Cassie could verbally assault the woman, Jess piped up. "We are trying to locate our friend Emma Lowell. Her mother-in-law is, or was, a resident here. Her last known whereabouts were here, forty-eight hours ago."

Mrs. Kozlowski nodded as she listened. "Well, you are correct. Mrs. Lowell is no longer living here. She has made other living arrangements, and her daughter-in-law was the person who was here when she checked out."

"Did anyone talk to Emma or Margaret to find out where they were going?"

"I'm afraid not. She didn't supply a forwarding address or any information as to what her plans were or where she was going."

"Wouldn't you normally find out something like that? I mean, these people need assistance. You can't just let them walk out the door like that."

"Actually, we can. They aren't here under doctor's orders or against their will. As long as a family member or other approved individual has them in their care when they leave, we don't usually pry into their personal lives."

"You're kidding me!" Cassie exclaimed.

"Isn't there anyone who was close to Margaret who might have heard something or maybe someone Margaret might have shared details of her plans with? Please?"

Mrs. Kozlowski chewed on her bottom lip for a moment then instructed Melissa to send out a page for a person named Jahaira.

"I'm about ready to freak out," Cassie shared quietly with Jess.

"I know, but we'll get more cooperation if we keep our cool. Let me handle this." Jess was glad she had someone with her, but Cassie needed to get a grip and not ruin their chance of getting information.

A pretty Latina, probably in her early twenties, approached the receptionist desk. "Yes, Miss K. You need to talk to me?" Her thick accent and halting English gave Jess immediate cause for concern. Was her English good enough that she would understand Margaret's plans after she left the care center?

"Thank you for coming so quickly, Jahaira. We need to ask some questions about Mrs. Lowell."

"Mrs. Lowell?"

"You remember Mrs. Lowell. Room 121. Margaret?"

"Oh yes. Margaret." The women clenched and unclenched her hands, licking her lips nervously.

Jess and Cassie exchanged glances. The fear on Jahaira's face was obvious.

"Did Mrs. Lowell ever share with you why she was leaving or where she was going?" Mrs. Kozlowski asked sternly.

"No," she shook her head. "She was lonely. Not many visitors."

"She must have said something about her plans, Jahaira," Mrs. Kozlowski questioned further.

Jahaira's forehead wrinkled as she thought about the question. "One day she say something about being a family again. She said her daughter would take care of her now."

"Her daughter?" Jess said. "You mean daughter-in-law?"

"Yes, maybe she say daughter-in-law."

"She didn't ever say where she was going? Never?" Cassie words were forceful, but she was keeping control.

"No." She was thoughtful for a moment. "One day she was looking at photos of a beautiful house. I asked if that was her home. She told me it was a . . ." She tapped her forehead trying to recall the information. "A home, in the mountains . . ."

"A cabin?" Cassie said loudly startling Jahaira.

The woman nodded quickly, flashing a frightened look at Mrs. Kozlowski.

"Is that where Margaret took her? That would explain her not having cell service," Jess asked, feeling hope that they'd found an explanation for Emma's sudden disappearance.

"But how in the world do we begin looking for her?" Cassie asked. "Mrs. Kozlowski, do you have any information about a cabin?"

"That's not information we need on file. The only thing I can think of is that you could contact Mrs. Lowell's attorney and see if he can help."

"Can we get that number and the address of his office?" Jess asked. Even though they finally had a lead, her sudden onset of anxiousness filled her with panic. The fact that Emma had left without notifying one of them, especially Landon, made the situation extremely suspicious.

While Melissa wrote down the information on a sticky note, Mrs. Kozlowski excused Jahaira, who hurried away without a backwards glance.

Melissa handed the paper to Jess.

"We appreciate your help," Jess told both women. "It's not like Emma to just take off without telling anyone, especially her fiancé."

"And the fact that she's with her mother-in-law," Cassie said. "I mean, let's be honest, Margaret Lowell isn't getting any Miss Congeniality awards anytime soon. The woman was cruel and demanding and made Emma's life very difficult when she was married to her son."

Mrs. Kozlowski listened, her expression blank, her eyes unblinking.

"Well," Jess said, "we'd better get going. Thank you again."

The director stood, transfixed for a moment, then, like snapping out of a trance, she said, "Why don't you leave a number where you can be reached. In case we think of anything else helpful."

Jess and Cassie wrote down their numbers for her then, without anything further to say, left the building.

By this time a steady rain was falling, and Jess pulled an umbrella from her purse. Huddling beneath the paisley print dome, they rushed to Cassie's car and got in.

"Okay, seriously, is it just me, or did the screeching music from the shower scene of *Psycho* keep playing through your head while we were in there?" Cassie asked.

"Something was weird; that's for sure."

"They know something," Cassie said. "More than they're telling us. That Jahaira woman looked terrified to speak."

"She did. It was a little creepy. I felt sorry for her."

"Well, let's go pay this attorney a visit. Hopefully he can help us." Cassie put the car in gear, turned the wipers on high and pulled out of the parking lot.

* * *

At one point during her sleep, Emma felt someone with her. Had Margaret come into her room? Had she administered other medications?

Emma fought for consciousness but wasn't stronger than the drugs. Reality and nightmares meshed. Awake or asleep she was consumed with fear and anger.

Having lost track of time, Emma prayed that daylight would come soon. With light came hope of a new day.

Her thoughts became clearer, and she realized she had to quit reacting and get control of her emotions. She had to remain calm.

Margaret had always been unreasonable in her demands and controlling and manipulative in her relationships, and according to Jonathan, she regularly took medication for some mental issues but never said what kind. Emma realized that whatever instabilities Margaret possessed had escalated to such a high level that Margaret had detached herself from logic and attached herself to crazy.

Trying to figure out the madness behind the actions gave Emma a sense of understanding, some kind of explanation for Margaret's behavior. Emma already knew that the death of Margaret's husband and then her son had pushed her to the edge, but it was clear Margaret had gone *over* the edge. She had planned and plotted and pulled off the ultimate charade to get Emma all to herself in a remote and inaccessible location. She'd invested a lot of time and preparation into creating the perfect plan, pretending to be sickly, pretending to be religious, and then waiting for just the right moment to launch it. She had also proven she was willing to do whatever it took to keep Emma there. That thought was the one that scared Emma the most.

When she and Landon first got engaged, she had been hesitant to tell Margaret. She knew it would upset the woman, and she actually feared that Margaret would flip out. On the day she told her, Margaret had seemed to handle the news with grace and charm. Now, thinking back, Emma thought she handled it too gracefully and too charmingly. Emma remembered walking out of the care center wondering what had just happened.

That must have been the calm before the storm.

A tingle of anger pushed away the fog in her brain. Margaret had been gathering information all along. Plotting, planning, preparing for this very moment. Margaret knew Landon was leaving for an extended period of time. She knew the storm was coming that would prevent them from leaving and prevent anyone to come looking for them. She managed to get out of the care center without notice. Who knew what she'd told them, but apparently, they were okay with it because they let her go.

Emma's fingers curled into a fist as her emotions surged; this was not going to happen. She was not going to let Margaret destroy her future.

Tears leaked from the corners of her eyes.

What could she do?

Heavenly Father. I can't believe this is happening. I need Thy help. This woman isn't well, I understand that, but I'm afraid of what she's going to do to me. Please show me what to do. Help me. Bless Landon too. I know he must be so worried. Stay with me, Father. I'm so scared.

She remembered how scared of thunder and lightning she'd been as a child. She would lie in bed at night, shivering with fear, counting until she heard the thunder after a flash of lightning. Closer and closer it would come until she would have the covers and her pillow over her head, while she trembled in fear, waiting for that ground shaking boom.

This was how she felt now, like she was waiting for thunder, knowing that any minute, something could happen.

A noise outside her room sent a shock of panic through her. Her instincts were right.

Pretending she was still under the influence of the medication, she listened as the door opened.

Emma's stomach turned inside out, and she broke out in a cold sweat. Now was not the time to throw up.

"Good morning, my dear. Did you sleep well?"

Emma didn't answer. She focused on her breathing, trying to stave off the nausea. The strange sweetness in Margaret's voice caused her to wonder if the woman had split personalities.

"Look at you, lying there so still, dressed in white." The woman laughed, the sound hollow and foreign. Emma was tempted to look to make sure it was Margaret. She didn't even sound like herself any longer.

"Yes, a white dress. Like little Penny Feinstein's dress that Easter. Pure white, with ribbons and ruffles, like a princess. So beautiful. Much more beautiful than mine. I wanted that dress, not that ridiculous green dress I was wearing."

Margaret's finger touched Emma's forearm; it took every ounce of restraint she had not to flinch. The woman stroked her arm.

"Of course, I couldn't let Penny overshadow me. No." She laughed. "I took care of her."

Margaret's hand rested on Emma's wrist. She circled her fingers around it and tightened her grip. "All that mud," she laughed, "against that pure white. And Penny's face," she loosened her grip. "'Oh, Penny, how clumsy of me. I'm so sorry.'" Margaret's tone was mocking. "Ha!"

Holding still as Margaret's touch traveled to Emma's cheek, Emma began to understand how disturbed Margaret was.

"My Jonathan always said you were the most beautiful woman he'd ever met." She chuckled. "His father said the same thing about me."

Her fingers then traced the line of Emma's jaw. "I guess you are beautiful in your own way. But he was mine, and you took him from me. He was mine to give, not yours to take. The day he married you was the worst day of my life."

She dug her nails into Emma's skin when she emphasized the word *worst*.

Emma turned her face away and made a soft groaning noise, as though her sleep had been interrupted. Inside she wanted to cry out at the pain of Margaret's biting nails.

"And now he's gone. And your beauty doesn't really matter. As much as I don't like it, I accept the fact that we are in this together. We don't have our sweethearts, but we have each other. We're all we've got. We've both lost the love of our lives, but we can take comfort knowing that we are devoting ourselves to their memory. Together.

"This robe of purity, the symbolic cutting of your hair to strip away vanity, the absence of your jewelry that represents your emotional obligations allows you to be free, to be your most raw, vulnerable self. Now, we can rebuild, now I can give you everything I own, and I can know that you will give me loyalty and companionship in return. This is all in preparation for something that we will do together." Margaret paused her strange narrative. Did she know Emma could hear her, or was she just that far removed from reality that it didn't matter whether she could or not?

"You see, my dear, Jonathan left something behind when he died."

He did? Emma couldn't think what it could be. All of his assets and belongings had been sorted and settled. The task had been easy because she gave almost everything to Margaret. All she kept were a few pieces of art that he'd given her as gifts.

"It belongs to us. You are the only one who can help me get it," she said, stroking Emma's cheek. "You will come to agree and accept this, and it will be just as it should be."

Her fingers left Emma's face. A light rustling at the nightstand next to the bed piqued Emma's interest. Knowing she had to keep her guard up, she opened her left eye just a slit. Margaret had her back turned, but even with her vision slightly blurred from the medication Margaret had given her, Emma saw what she was doing.

Taking the lid off a bottled water, Margaret pulled a pill capsule apart and poured the contents into it. She put the lid back on and gave the bottle a shake.

So, she was just going to keep Emma drugged until she conformed, was that her plan?

Emma's mouth was dry from whatever other drugs Margaret had given her, and Margaret probably knew that. She also knew that Emma would drink the bottled water, since there was no other water available to her.

Thirst and hunger were beginning to besiege her body, but Emma would never drink that water. She needed to keep her wits sharp.

Reasoning with Margaret would never be an option. The disturbed woman had snapped.

She would never accept this or conform. She would have to get fluids somehow and then find clothes and sneak away.

It was a long shot, but she was not going to lie there and be a victim. She would either escape to freedom or die trying.

"Sleep well, my darling. Soon, very soon, you will understand why I'm doing this. And you will thank me."

Remaining perfectly still until Margaret left the room, Emma continued to pretend to sleep. Confusion at Margaret's words gave her greater reason for concern. She had to get away as soon as possible.

Escape options played through her mind. Luckily she'd been through the house enough to have a general knowledge of the layout. She remembered a coat closet near the front door that possibly had overclothes. She would need to sneak into the kitchen while Margaret was asleep, which was when she could check the closet. She would do it tonight. Once she figured out everything she needed, then she could decide when to escape.

Playing along with Margaret's plan to brainwash and keep her captive, Emma carefully moved from the bed so there was no noise and took the water bottle to the bathroom sink and poured most of it down the drain. Still feeling flu-like, she prayed she wouldn't throw up. This was no place to get dehydrated.

Holding her mouth under the faucet, she turned the handle, and a tiny stream of water trickled into her mouth before running out. It was enough to moisten her throat and relieve the dryness.

She took a moment to look at each of her shoulders, locating the painful, swollen red area where Margaret had given her shots. What medications was she giving her? Emma knew that somehow she needed to avoid getting any more injections or pills.

But right now, more than anything, she needed a drink. Then a thought occurred to her. She looked through the cabinets and drawers for a container, but they'd all been emptied. She took the silk flowers out of a small vase on the windowsill and shoved them into a drawer. Standing on the toilet she was able to open the small window and scoop snow from the windowsill into the vase.

Closing the window as quietly as she could, she took the vase back to the bed with her. Emma felt weakened and tired from lack of food and water and from the medication Margaret had given her.

She climbed back onto the bed and listened through the stillness, trying to hear any noise from Margaret, in case Margaret decided to pay her a surprise visit.

Feeling the jagged edges of her hair and the hollowness of her stomach, Emma rolled onto her side and said another prayer for guidance and help. It would be easy to freak out and panic, but she felt surprisingly calm. That feeling of calm gave her the reassurance that she wasn't alone. God was aware of her and He was with her, and even more importantly, she knew He would help her.

On her nightstand was the Bible Margaret had given her. Even though she was familiar with the story of Ruth and Naomi, she hadn't really studied it.

With nothing else to do in her prison, she picked up the book and opened it to the book of Ruth and began reading while she slowly ate the snow in the vase.

* * *

"Out of business! This can't be happening!" Cassie kicked the door of the vacant office where Margaret's attorney was supposed to be practicing.

"The operator said there isn't an attorney by that name listed," Jess told her as she hung up from speaking with information.

"What's going on, Jess? There is something horribly wrong happening."

"I know. What do we do now?"

"We'd better go to the police. Maybe they've got something on Margaret or the Lowell family that would be helpful." Cassie fumbled for her keys in her pocket.

"I agree. This is bigger than we are. I need to call Landon and let him know what's going on."

"Wait till we talk to the police, when we know more. He's likely to get on the next plane home when we tell him what's going on."

Just as Jess was putting her cell phone in her pocket, it vibrated. She looked at the number but didn't recognize it.

Jess and Cassie looked at each other then Jess answered the call.

"Hello?"

"Hello. This is Melissa, from Whispering Pines."

Jess's mouth dropped open. Cassie noticed her reaction, and her eyes grew wide.

"Who is it?" Cassie asked.

"Melissa from the care center," Jess whispered.

"Oh," Cassie mouthed, nodding her head. "Put her on speaker phone."

Jess touched the screen, and Melissa's voice came through the speaker.

"I had to wait for my break to call you," she said. "First of all, I need to make sure that what I tell you won't get back to Mrs. Kozlowski and that you will keep it between us."

"Of course, Melissa," Jess said.

"Okay. Because I could lose my job over this, and I can't afford to have that happen."

"I understand. Your information is safe with me."

"Good. Thank you."

Melissa went silent.

"Melissa?"

"Sorry, I was just checking to make sure no one is watching. I came out to my car to call you. So, here's what I know. First of all, I think it's important that you know that recently Mrs. Lowell had a psychiatric review done on her. Her behavior had gotten, um, I guess the best way to put it is, out of control: violence, anger, treating the employees here horribly, throwing her trays of food on the floor, treating the other residents horribly, stuff like that."

"Wow, that's kind of scary."

"It was. Jahaira, the woman you met, was terrified of her, yet for some reason Margaret liked her. She was the only employee Margaret would tolerate in her room. I think it was because Jahaira's English isn't really good, and Margaret knew she couldn't repeat a lot of what she said."

"That makes sense."

"Anyway, the doctors issued a diagnosis and also recommended that she receive extensive treatment and counseling. Even possibly moving her to a psychiatric facility where she could be watched more closely.

Of course, when Margaret heard this, she went completely ballistic. I'm telling you, I could hear the screaming all the way from her room, and her room was on the other side of the facility."

"Do you know what her diagnosis was?" Jess asked.

"No, I don't usually have access to reports and personal patient information. But it must have been bad because she didn't waste time making arrangements to leave Whispering Pines, and we couldn't force her to seek help for her problems. She somehow convinced everyone that her daughter-in-law was willing to take care of her and help manage her affairs, so once all the paperwork was signed and she was released from Whispering Pines, we had no further obligation to her."

"But Emma would never sign an agreement to have full control and responsibility for Margaret. She's engaged to be married. If anything, she wanted to distance herself from Margaret as much as possible."

"That explains Margaret's speed in taking care of the situation. Her attorney came in to see her the very next day. And when he turned his visitor's badge in and left the facility after their meeting, I'm serious, the guy was white as a sheet. I thought maybe he was sick or something. Did you get a hold of him?"

"No, his phone has been disconnected and his office has been vacated," Jess told her.

"I looked through the file to find out anything that might be helpful for you because I think you have every reason to be worried for your friend. That woman is psycho. She may be bound to a wheelchair, but that doesn't stop her from terrorizing everyone around her."

"You didn't find anything about a cabin, or another person we could contact?"

"Her only other living relative is her sister, who lives back East. I jotted down her number in case you want to talk to her."

"Yes! I do! Melissa, I can't thank you enough."

"If I find out anything else, I will get in touch."

"Please do."

"Good luck finding your friend."

* * *

"Emma? I have something for you to drink."

Margaret's voice startled her awake. "What!" she exclaimed, pushing herself up onto her elbows.

"There, there, dear. Calm down. I brought you some water."

Emma relaxed onto the pillow but didn't respond.

"You need to drink, dear."

"Just leave it," Emma said. "I don't feel well. I'm sick. I think I have the flu."

A flicker of a smile caught the edges of Margaret's mouth then she said, "All the more reason you should drink. Here, let me help you." Margaret reached for her, but Emma recoiled and put her hands up to stop her.

"I will when I'm ready." She kept her eyes diverted from Margaret, hoping to play upon her sympathies.

She felt Margaret's gaze on her.

"You know, Emma, I am not trying to hurt you, but you have forced me to do this. I couldn't let you remarry. I had to do something to stop you before you made such a big mistake."

Emma didn't answer. Her thoughts were consumed with wondering if Landon had made it safely, if he knew she was missing, if she'd ever survive this.

"It will be worth it. You have so much to gain. If you were to marry that man, I would be forced to remove you from my will. Someday, when I'm gone you will be a very rich woman. But you will also have something even greater than all the money I could give you.

"You see, we've both been given a gift from Jonathan. All I ask is that you pledge your devotion to Jonathan and to me until the day I pass away. After that, well, after that, I guess I have no say in the matter."

What in the world was she talking about? What was this gift?

She was tempted to tell Margaret that she didn't want a dime of her money, but again, she knew better than to try and have any sort of normal discussion with the woman. It was Margaret's way or no way. Emma had to wait for the right opportunity.

"Emma, did you hear me?"

Emma mumbled some words to emphasize the fact that she was in a weakened, drug induced state. Two could play at this game. Up to this point Margaret had faked her illnesses and injuries to seem pathetic and weak, using a wheelchair and a walker, appearing so feeble and frail.

Ha! Emma was onto her, and she planned to overexaggerate how she was feeling. She was determined to give an Oscar-worthy performance.

"Hmm." Margaret placed her hand on Emma's forehead then she felt her cheek. "Your color isn't good." She found Emma's wrist and checked her pulse.

Genetically Emma had a low resting heart rate and low blood pressure. She wished she could say it was because she avidly worked out, but it was something she was born with. Doctors were always astounded at her stats. This wasn't something Margaret knew, which explained her concern.

However, the clamminess of her skin was due to the occasional hot flashes she was having, followed by chills. She didn't know what was going on. This was unlike any flu she'd ever experienced.

"Emma, you need to drink some water." She shook Emma's shoulder.

Playing the victim part to perfection, Emma moaned like she was in pain, hugging herself and pulling her knees into the fetal position. The fact of the matter was that not only was she sick, but she also hadn't eaten since the morning she'd taken Landon to the airport. The small amounts of snow she'd eaten hadn't hydrated her enough to satisfy her and wouldn't sustain her much longer.

Margaret jiggled Emma's shoulder. "Emma, you need to wake up." Emma enjoyed knowing the woman was concerned. "Oh dear, what have I done?" Margaret rushed from the room.

Ha! Gotcha! Emma thought. Margaret deserved everything she was getting.

Hopefully the woman would bring her back some food. She was hungry enough she would risk eating it.

Trying to formulate a game plan, she heard commotion below and knew that Margaret was in the kitchen doing something.

She had to outsmart her at her own game. Play along. Convince Margaret that she was coming around, accepting the arrangement.

But over her dead body would she ever accept this! After hearing Margaret's revelation of her strong feelings against Emma when she married Jonathan, she knew the woman's state of mind. Especially when she revealed how, even as a child, she had to have things her way and would do whatever she had to get it. Even to the extent of throwing mud on a little girl's dress because she couldn't bear someone having something better than her. The woman had deep issues and was dangerous. The sooner Emma got out of there, the better.

It was interesting to reflect back on her experiences with Margaret and all the times she'd thought Margaret's actions were controlling, manipulative, and crazy. Of course, she could have never expressed it to Jonathan, but she had always felt Margaret was off her rocker. She just had no idea the woman had gone completely off the deep end into the chasm of pure crazy.

Footsteps sounding on the stairs caused her stomach muscle to tighten. She didn't know what to expect from one moment to the next.

Emma opened her eyes, remaining motionless, watching as Margaret entered the room with a tray. She kept her gaze empty, not letting her eyes betray her emotions. She wanted to appear as blank and numb as she could. Keeping her emotions out of the situation would give her the upper hand; she would never let Margaret know she was getting to her.

"It is time for you to eat, my dear. You have behaved well, and you shall be rewarded."

Emma didn't show a response.

Finding space for the tray on the top of the dresser, Margaret carried a bowl to the bed and sat on the edge. "Here you go. Some broth will help you get your strength."

At first Emma had a mind to resist, but hunger won out, along with a desire to have nourishment so she could have the strength and clarity to carry out her escape plan.

Feeding small spoonfuls to Emma, Margaret said, "This reminds me of my days at the hospital. Not that I enjoyed being a nurse all that much. I mean, really, who wants to take care of whiny, sick people all day long? I got my nursing degree so I could marry a doctor. My plan worked like a charm."

She dabbed the corners of Emma's lips with a napkin. The chicken broth was like manna. Emma closed her eyes as the salty liquid trickled down the back of her throat.

"Oh no you don't; no sleeping. Time for you to wake up."

Emma opened her eyes.

"There now, you're getting some color back into your face." She gave her another spoonful of broth. "How are you feeling?"

Not wanting to engage in a conversation with her captor, Emma just shrugged her shoulders. Her dry mouth, fatigue, lightheadedness, and blurred vision were just a few of her complaints.

"You should be perking up a little now that you've had something to eat. I might have overdone the Cyclobenzaprine just a tad. Or was it the Lupron?"

The drugs had names. Too bad Emma had no idea what they were.

When Margaret had decided she'd fed Emma enough, she put the bowl aside and offered her a drink from a bottle of water. Emma shook her head and looked away.

"Fine, I'll leave this here. It will be nice when we can enjoy meals together. We need to start building your strength and making you healthy. You have something very important ahead of you."

Emma knew the alarm she felt inside registered on her face. Something bizarre was going through Margaret's head.

"Very soon you will know, and you will thank me."

Picking up the tray, Margaret stepped toward the door. "Until then, the more I can trust you, the more freedom you'll have. Don't let me down."

Emma looked away as she left the room. She was determined to keep her focus and not let Margaret control her.

Feeling stronger from the small amount of food, she thought through her plan again. She had to move slowly and take her time so she didn't alert Margaret to her actions. Who knew what would happen if Margaret didn't feel she could trust Emma. She had to get everything in place and then make her escape happen on the first try. She wouldn't have another chance; she was certain Margaret would see to that.

Drifting in and out of sleep, drinking melted snow and trying to stay calm when she was often on the verge of freaking out, Emma hovered between dreams and reality, a constant prayer flowing through her mind.

When she felt strong enough to stand, she went to the window and watched the shadows grow longer on the thick blanket of snow, blending into darkness.

Shivering she crawled back into bed, under the covers. The thin cotton gown provided no warmth against the winter chill. With no warm clothing or food to give her fuel to heat her body, she couldn't get warm.

She climbed into bed just in time. Footsteps on the stairs warned of Margaret's imminent entrance.

8

"HELLO?" A FEEBLE VOICE SAID on the other end of the phone.

"Is this Mary Philips?"

"Yes, who's calling, please?"

"My name is Jessica Wilson. My friend Emma was married to your sister's son, Jonathan."

"My sister!"

Jess heard the immediate anger in her voice. She quickly put the phone on speaker.

"Yes. I'm trying to locate Emma. The last time anyone saw her she was with your sister two days ago."

"As far as I'm concerned, I have no sister."

"I'm sorry if this is difficult for you. But we are very worried about our friend. It's not like her to just disappear without telling anyone."

"If she's with Margaret, she's probably being held against her will."

"Why do you say that?"

"No one would spend time with that woman just because they wanted to. She's a horrible, mean, vindictive woman who is very unhappy and only finds joy when she knows other people are suffering.

"She abandoned me when I needed her the most, and she has only caused me pain and grief in my life. The only way I've been able to deal with it is to just remove her from my life."

"I am so sorry for the heartache you've had. I just wondered if I could ask you a few questions."

"I suppose so, if it's to help you and your friend. If it's to help Margaret, then no, I won't answer any questions."

"Believe me, we are concerned about our friend."

"All right then, I'll see if I can help."

"Two days ago your sister checked out of the Whispering Pines Care Center. She was with our friend, Emma. No one has seen her since. We can't figure out where they might have gone. Mrs. Lowell's house was sold over a year ago, and she has no living relatives in the area, as far as we know."

"We only have a few relatives, but none of them live on the West Coast," Mary said.

"We found out that the Lowells had a cabin somewhere. We're wondering if maybe that's where they went. Do you know anything about this cabin?"

"I recall hearing that they had one. She has always been competitive with me for some reason, and when they first bought the cabin, she gloated and bragged about it. You see, my husband was a very wealthy man, and Margaret couldn't handle the fact that I had more money than she did. She pushed her poor husband to his death to provide her with everything she felt she deserved. She would drive anyone to suicide!"

"Do you know where the cabin is?"

"She never invited me to come to the cabin, but I do know where it is because she bragged in great detail about it. It's in the Cascades, on the south of the Skykomish River. I think once you get in the area you could ask around. People would know where the Lowell cabin is because it was extremely large and ostentatious. I'm sure people think the Lowells are horrible snobs, and they would be right!"

Jess had heard of sibling rivalry, but this was going pretty far.

"I can't thank you enough for your help, Mary. Is there anything else you can think of that might be helpful?" she said.

"I just want to warn you that my sister doesn't seem to have a conscience when it comes to getting her way. People and their feelings mean nothing to her. My parents did not raise her to be this way, but she seemed driven to please only herself and get her way, no matter what the cost. I remember watching her treat her friends like dirt and discarding boys like garbage when she grew tired of them."

Jess drummed her fingers, willing the woman to finish talking. They'd found out all they needed to hear, and she felt every moment mattered in their efforts to find Emma.

"She had this control over people, and she manipulated them like puppets. For some reason, other school kids wanted to be her friend, even when they saw how horribly she treated people. I remember when she was in ninth grade she started dating Gavin Reynolds, the most popular and good-looking boy in school. He did everything he could to please her and acted like a moron because of her. Then a new kid moved into our school . . . Dean Parker. He wasn't as handsome as Gavin, but he had a great sense of humor and charisma, and kids liked him immediately, especially my sister."

Jess rolled her eyes, and Cassie lifted both hands up helplessly. The woman wouldn't stop talking.

"She dumped Gavin like a bag of rocks and focused all her attention on Dean. Gavin was devastated. He was so depressed he quit the basketball team then quit coming to school. He even tried to commit suicide by taking a bottle of prescription pills, but his sister found him in time, thank goodness. Their family moved after that. My sister, Margaret, didn't even care. She said he was an idiot and deserved to die."

Jess swallowed hard. Cassie's mouth dropped open.

"This is the type of person you're dealing with. She is dangerous when she feels threatened. Please be careful."

Jess felt queasy at the thought of Emma being with this unstable and completely psychotic woman. She didn't care what it took—they were going to find their friend!

* * *

"Good evening," Margaret announced in a cheery voice. "Have you had a nice rest today?"

Emma couldn't help looking at her like she was crazy. The woman talked as if Emma were on vacation and she was the owner of a bed and breakfast.

"I brought you some toast. I figured you might like something a bit more substantial."

Eyeing the toast on the plate Margaret set on the bed beside her, Emma wasn't sure if she dared to eat it. She feared Margaret was playing a trick on her or testing her somehow.

Tentatively she reached for the top piece of buttered toast, watching Margaret constantly, preparing for the woman to smack her on the hand or stab her with a needle or something.

Margaret just looked on with pleasure as Emma took a small bite and licked the smear of butter from her upper lip.

"Good, isn't it?"

Emma nodded slightly and took another bite.

"That's a good girl. You need some meat on your bones. You're awfully thin. We need to get you strong and healthy. You have an important duty ahead of you." She sat in the chair next to the window. "The first time Jonathan introduced us I remember thinking how thin you were. He'd always dated girls with nice full figures. I worried about you being able to give him children."

Good grief! Emma wasn't about to have this discussion with her. Margaret was trying to convince her that the reason they didn't have children was because of her weight. She'd tried to get Jonathan to go to a fertility specialist with her to find out why they couldn't conceive, but according to him, he was above the possibility that *HE* couldn't produce children. Feeling it was her fault, she went through a battery of tests without his knowledge, wanting desperately to know if it was because of her that they hadn't had children. The doctor looked her square in the eye after the results came back and told her not only was she healthy and strong but she was also perfectly capable of conceiving and bearing children. Funny, how even now, she remembered how she kept the information from Jonathan to spare herself the reaction she knew she would get from him. This was the same reason she didn't tell Margaret. It just wasn't worth it. Besides, Margaret would think what she wanted no matter what Emma told her.

Bottom line was, as soon as she escaped this cabin of craziness, she would make sure Margaret spent the remainder of her days in jail. Emma vowed she would never have contact with Margaret again, no matter how much money or inheritance she had to forfeit. Nothing was worth this madness.

Eating slowly, but wanting to devour both pieces of toast, she listened to Margaret's constant blabbering about her perfect son and their imperfect marriage and how she was giving Emma a second chance to prove herself worthy of her dead husband. Her devotion in his death would absolve her of her imperfections and whatever she lacked when he was alive.

As Margaret explained her reasoning and the joy they would share together, unified in their devotion to their dead husbands and their shared bond, Emma had a deeper understanding of how disturbed Margaret was. She began to fear that Margaret was so convinced of this concept that she would be willing to do anything to prevent Emma from remarrying or from leaving her.

To escape would be perilous, even deadly. Margaret appeared to have an arsenal of drugs at her disposal. Who knew what she would administer to punish her, or kill her.

But Emma was willing to risk it. She was weak, but a surge of energy and determination grew slowly inside her. Gone was the girl who was willing to conform and allow herself to be manipulated and backed into a corner. She would rather die trying to escape than endure this insanity any longer. She had nothing to lose and everything to gain. Tonight when Margaret was in bed, she would go through the house and formulate her plan.

"Now, isn't that better?" Margaret took the plate from Emma's lap and placed it on the tray.

Emma nodded.

Margaret looked intensely at her and smiled satisfactorily. "Your countenance is already changing. I am pleased. Trust me, Emma. This will all be worth it. I have something of a surprise in store for you. When I know you are ready, I will tell you."

Emma couldn't conjure up a smile. The pleased look on Margaret's face nauseated her.

Margaret sat on the edge of the bed and took one of Emma's hands in hers, the bony coldness of her fingers sending chills up Emma's spine.

"My days are numbered, my dear. Knowing that you will be with me and we will share something wonderful brings great peace to my soul."

Even with all Margaret had done to her, Emma couldn't have a heart of stone. Was the woman really dying?

"How do you know that your days are numbered?" she asked.

"I am certain my heart is failing. It's what took my mother and eventually will take my horrid sister."

Emma had only met Margaret's sister once, but her impression was the complete opposite. She remembered how warm and caring she was, and she remembered how Mary had taken her hands in hers, looked her in the eye and said, "I hope you can be happy, and if you ever need anything, I hope you will call me."

Her words had haunted Emma when Jonathan's and Margaret's true natures were revealed. Mary had known at the beginning that happiness would be difficult, even impossible. Thinking back, Emma wished she had called Mary. Who knew, things might have turned out differently.

"I know I won't live much longer. That's why I'm so anxious to take care of loose ends before I go. I've been waiting for the right moment to bring you here, planning and waiting . . ."

Emma listened intently, curious to hear what had gone into Margaret's reasoning for what she was doing.

"I knew it had to happen before you made the biggest mistake of your life and married that oaf of a fiancé of yours."

Emma didn't react on the outside, but inside she was seething at the comment.

"And of course, with my health declining so rapidly, I knew it was time."

Emma fought every impulse to lash out and kept control of her emotions. Margaret was testing her. The sooner she learned to play the game, the better she could beat her at it.

"Isn't there something you can do? Medicine? A transplant?" Emma asked, trying to act concerned, hoping it was convincing.

Margaret's face softened, and she patted Emma's hand. "No dear. Not at my age."

"I had no idea."

"Well, I didn't want to burden you."

Emma nearly burst out laughing. Who did she think she was kidding? That seemed to be all she wanted to do. In fact, now that she was seeing this new side of Margaret, she wondered how many of the past ailments and emergencies had been fabricated. And now this heart problem? Was it even true?

Margaret cried wolf so much Emma didn't know what to think or believe. Instinct told her to believe nothing and suspect everything.

"I'll let you rest now. You have been through a lot. I am sure you are worn out."

"Can I do anything to help you?" Emma asked. Her mother had always taught her when she had a problem with a friend to "kill them with kindness." Would that work now?

With a slow shake of her head, her expression beaming, Margaret said, "That is so sweet of you. I'm actually doing well today. Thank you, my dear. So lovely of you to ask."

Emma smiled, hoping to convey caring and concern in spite of her complete dislike for the woman.

"It is amazing to see you out of your wheelchair and not using a walker," Emma said.

Margaret laughed with an undeniable tone of deviousness, "Yes, well, that's one thing I learned about old age. People will do just about anything for an elderly person in a wheelchair. I needed it for a few days after my stroke, but it was such a mild stroke I didn't really need it much after that. However, it became a very useful tool in helping me carry out my plan for us." Margaret nodded satisfactorily, obviously pleased with herself.

Emma was speechless and knew anything she said would set the woman off and ruin the progress she'd made in convincing Margaret that she was coming around to her way of thinking. Emma knew that understanding her opponent would help her win.

"We'll talk again in the morning. Perhaps we can spend some time together. I brought some wonderful home movies of Jonathan when he was a baby. You won't believe how adorable he was." Her voice cracked, and she placed her hand on her chest. "How I miss him."

There was a moment of silence while Margaret got caught up in her emotions and Emma watched her. The woman still struggled with her son's death. Emma couldn't deny that her former mother-in-law loved and missed her son. Is that what had caused her to snap?

* * *

"Thank you, officer. I'll watch for your call," Jess said when she ended the conversation. She stuffed her phone into her back pocket.

"Well?" Cassie shoved a french fry loaded with ketchup into her mouth. "What did he say?"

Jess stared at Cassie chomping away on her food and remembered how, when she was a child, her mother had been a stickler on manners and constantly reminded her about not talking with her mouth full. As a kid she hadn't understood the big deal. She felt like calling her mother and thanking her for teaching her manners.

"The officer said there is no crime of being missing and that if a person is voluntarily missing, they are entitled to their privacy."

"Which means?"

"Somehow we have to prove that Emma has been forcibly taken."

"How? What do they need? You told him she was getting married soon, right?"

"I did. He said people bail all the time before a wedding for dozens of reasons."

Cassie closed her eyes and groaned. "What about her mother-in-law being crazy?"

"He said we need to prove—"

Their eyes connected.

"We need Melissa's help to prove Margaret is certifiably nuts," Cassie said.

"I'll call her right now."

Melissa figured out a way to get them a copy of Margaret's records and the report, but she would need to stay at work until five so as not to raise suspicion. They arranged a time to meet, and as soon as they had the report, they could take it to the police department.

Jess sighed. "I hate just sitting here. I am so worried about Emma."

"I am too, especially after talking to her sister. Margaret sounds like a psycho." Cassie went back to eating fries and polished off one small paper tub of ketchup and started on another one. She noticed Jess watching her.

"Is something wrong?"

"Huh?" Jess shook her head to clear the fog from being lost in thought. She realized that the way Cassie ate her fries was exactly how Sean had eaten them. He had loved ketchup, which was weird because he hated tomatoes.

"I asked if there was something wrong," Cassie said, wiping her mouth. "You're watching me eat my fries, and you have this weird, disapproving look on your face."

Jess didn't know what caught her off guard the most—that Cassie could perceive her expression so accurately or that she actually called her on it.

"It's nothing."

"Jess, I can tell something is bothering you. If there is, I want you to tell me."

"Okay, well, I was watching how much ketchup you put on your fries and was trying to remember who it was that liked that much ketchup, then I suddenly remembered . . . it was Sean."

"Sean?" Cassie had one side of her face scrunched up as she thought. "The only guy I know named Sean was from . . ."

"High school."

"Right. He did like ketchup. In fact, he was crazy about condiments. It was the weirdest thing. I don't really know what his fascination was, but he was really obsessed with condiments. I mean, he kept ketchup packages in his car . . ."

Jess just looked at her, not joining Cassie's walk down memory lane.

"I think I'm missing something here," Cassie said. "Did I say something to upset you?"

Jess felt it was against her better judgment to say anything, but she decided if Cassie could be so open, then she could unload some of the baggage she'd been carrying around since high school.

"It's just hard to hear you be so open about your relationship with Sean when you have to know how badly that hurt me when you stole him from me." The words just tumbled from her mouth completely bypassing her brain. She'd said it. And even though she was completely over Sean, it felt good to get it out.

Cassie's expression shifted from surprise, to shock, and finally to confusion. "I'm sorry, what did you just say?"

"I said, it's hard—"

"Wait a minute." Cassie's narrowed gaze and furrowed brow deepened the incredulous tone of her voice. "You seriously think I stole him from you?"

"Yes. Because you totally did."

Cassie nodded a few times, taking in a full, deep breath and letting it out slowly.

Jess was puzzled by her reaction. Was she going to deny it?

Cassie closed her eyes, steadying her breathing. After a moment she asked, "Is that what you've thought all these years?" She opened her eyes and riveted her gaze on Jess's face.

"I was there, Cassie. I know what happened."

"Wow," she said, slumping back, "that explains so much."

"What do you mean by that?"

"You were the only other female member of the Church in our school, and I wanted to be friends with you, but right off the bat you were very cold to me. Actually, you were more rude than cold. I had no idea why you didn't like me, but I could tell you didn't, so I decided to stay out of your way."

"You stole my boyfriend!"

Cassie was clearly taken aback. She stared at Jess with her mouth open. Then she closed it, cleared her throat, and said, "If you two were boyfriend and girlfriend, then it's news to me because he never said anything about you dating seriously. Ever. I even asked him because a few people said you two were dating. I asked him if it was serious, and he said no. He told me you were just friends and hung out together."

"He said we were just friends?" Jess didn't believe her.

Cassie looked Jess directly in the eyes and said, "Jess, I promise. I'm not that kind of a person. I would never, ever do something like that. If I had known you two were dating, I would have backed off."

"If you had come to me, I would have told you."

"I tried. Don't you remember? Right after I moved in they were having that seminary dance, and I thought it would be a good idea to go and get to know other members. I called you thinking maybe we could go together because I thought we could be friends. I was so excited to have a girl my age in my ward."

Jess had a vague recollection of the phone conversation.

"You told me that you were going with some friends and that the car was full. The only other person I knew was Sean, so I called him. That was our first night hanging out. A couple of people at the dance said something about you, so I asked him if you two were a couple and he said, no. To be honest, the more I hung out with Sean, the more I realized he was kind of a jerk. We were friends, but I never wanted to date him seriously. He was really caught up in himself, you know. I don't really go for guys with big egos."

Cassie was right; Sean had been conceited in high school. He was a big shot athlete, and he was good-looking. Cassie had enough self-esteem to see through that. Jess, on the other hand, had liked being known as the girl dating him.

When Cassie had moved into her ward, Jess remembered feeling threatened by her. Then when Cassie and Sean became friends, she had become protective and defensive. When she'd confronted Sean about dating Cassie, he had told her that now that his mission was getting closer, he felt it was important to not get serious with one girl and he hoped they could stay friends. What a load of compost!

She covered her face with her hands. All this time she'd blamed Cassie for her own insecurities and assumptions. Cassie had done nothing wrong. Sean was the one to blame!

"Jess, are you okay?"

"I'm just realizing what a jerk and an idiot I was in high school."

"What? No you weren't. Everyone who knew you always said nice things about you. I just figured you had a problem with me. Sean was smooth; a lot of girls like that. I just happen to not be one of them."

"Cassie"—Jess looked up at her—"I'm so sorry. I feel so badly about how I treated you. I was jealous of you because you were so pretty and confident and the boy who I thought was my boyfriend liked you."

"Seriously, Jess, it's no big deal. Things worked out the way they were supposed to. Luckily neither of us ended up with him. I hear he's been divorced twice. No surprise there."

"You forgive me?"

"There's nothing to forgive. I just hope we can put it all behind us and be friends."

Jess smiled at her. "I'd like that."

"Good," Cassie said, shoving the empty food containers onto a tray. "Let's go meet Melissa. It's time to find our friend."

* * *

The ticking of the clock through the evening stillness gave Emma a sense of calm. There had been no sound of movement, just Margaret's snoring, which Emma heard from across the hallway. Surely it was safe to get up now.

Stepping onto the ice-cold hardwood floor that sent a chill through her, Emma moved cautiously, hesitantly, not wanting the boards beneath her feet to squeak or move.

Her nerves were raw, her stomach crawling with anxiety. She half expected Margaret to come tearing into her room with a chainsaw or an ax. She'd never liked horror movies. In high school when her friends had gone to see the latest Halloween terror flick, she'd passed. Little did she know she would be living her own nightmare one day.

In her mind she had a dialogue with Jonathan, expressing to him her shock and dismay at his mother.

Why didn't you warn me? Why didn't you ever defend me to her? I was nothing but devoted and loving, willing to do whatever I needed to do to be a good wife. What did I do to deserve you being unfaithful and your mother being unhappy with me?

The unanswered questions fueled her anger, igniting her spirit of survival. She'd given up four years of her life to this family, and most of that time was spent trying to figure out what she was doing wrong and how to be happy again. Now, with Landon, she had found complete and true happiness. She had never felt so loved and cherished in her life. A sense of security and peace filled her soul. She had the gospel, and she had Landon. Whatever the future held, she was ready to face it with optimism and hope.

But first she had to get away from Margaret.

She tested the knob, which, of course, was locked. Quickly and carefully in the dark, she went into the bathroom and slid open the top drawer in the vanity. She'd done a thorough search of the bathroom when she was looking for a container for melting snow. The cupboard and drawers had been cleaned out completely except for one bobby pin, wedged in the back of the top drawer, almost impossible to see.

She'd examined the lock earlier and realized it was a simple button lock mechanism. With trembling hands, she straightened the bobby pin, hoping it would do the trick.

A storm was raging outside, and there was no moonlight. She felt around for the small hole where she needed to insert the bobby pin. Keeping her breath steady, she forced herself to stay focused and calm.

Working in the dark allowed her to tune in completely to her task, and when she felt the inserted pin grab hold of something, she knew it was going to open. With a determined push, Emma felt the pin hit the tiny mechanism inside, and the lock button on the other side popped.

Fear struck her heart, and she froze, praying the noise didn't wake Margaret.

Margaret's snoring stopped, and Emma prepared to bolt for her bed. Relief filled her when the snoring started again.

She decided to wait before attempting to leave the room, just to make sure Margaret was really asleep.

The fury of the storm outside helped create a background noise that she hoped would drown out any sound she made. She was tired of waiting. It was time to get out of this place.

Slowly she rotated the doorknob then pulled. The door opened. But the excitement was overshadowed by her fear of getting caught.

Tiptoeing out of the room she stopped, held her breath, and listened. Margaret's door was shut, but Emma assumed the woman was probably a light sleeper, especially with a prisoner across the hall.

One careful, silent step after another took her down the hallway. She thought about the situation, unable to believe all this was really happening. She should be able to reason with Margaret, tell her that she'd gone too far and people just didn't do things like this. But Margaret wasn't rational. Her actions and her thinking were beyond reason.

Gripping the banister as she descended the stairs, Emma tried to land each step without noise. When she arrived at the bottom, she released the breath she'd held the entire way down.

The first thing she did was check the closet inside the front door. Just as she suspected, there were several parkas and sets of snow pants, good quality for snowmobiling. If she could find boots, gloves, and a hat, she would be in business.

Outside the wind blew, the moonlight covered by storm clouds. Snow was falling again. She shivered then continued on her mission. Feeling with her hands, she located a basket on the shelf above the coat rack, and to her relief she found gloves and several thick, fleecy hats.

Instinct told her to check the floor, and sure enough, she found several pairs of boots. They would be too big, but she would make do. Anything but barefoot would work.

Now the last thing to do was locate her purse and clothing, but she guessed they were in Margaret's room. How did she get them out of there? And the even bigger question, did it make sense to leave right now?

The fierceness of the storm beat at the windows. Not only was it dark, but there was a blizzard. If she got lost, she would freeze. If she couldn't see her way, she could easily walk off a cliff.

She wanted to leave, but she wanted to be smart. Now that she had a game plan, she would hope and pray that the skies were clear the next night.

Then she had a thought, why not just leave during the day? If she could drug Margaret, she could leave while the sun was shining. All she needed to do was find Margaret's stash of drugs. Somehow she would find a way to knock the woman out and sneak away. The powerful drugs would keep her sedated for at least eight hours.

In the kitchen she began to open cupboards, hoping to locate the supply of medicine Margaret had. The only thing of value she found was a packet of saltine crackers. She would hide them in her room and eat them. She didn't dare take much because she feared Margaret would notice it.

Frustrated, she felt around. It had to be here somewhere. She walked toward the other side of the kitchen, jamming her little toe into a footstool off to the side of the refrigerator. Throbbing pain forced her to her knees. She grabbed her injured toe and took deep breaths. The last time she did this, she'd broken her pinky toe.

After a moment the pain subsided enough that she could stand. She wanted to throw the footstool across the room. Then she realized—that stool hadn't been there earlier; Margaret had moved it there. What was she keeping in the cupboard above the fridge?

Moving the stool into position, she climbed on top and opened the cupboard.

Jackpot! She found bottles and vials of medications, a small pharmaceutical stash that would take down a herd of elephants. She wasn't sure why Margaret was keeping the meds up there; she was just glad she found them.

In the darkness, she had no idea what any of the drugs were. Grabbing two of the bottles that were right at the front, she opened the lids and took four pills out of each one. It was a guessing game at this point, but she was left with no choice.

The creak of a bed overhead sent a shock of terror through Emma's heart.

Please, Father, protect me. Please don't let her wake up and find me.

She'd never prayed so much or so long in her life. In fact, whenever she was awake, she was praying.

She quickly put the bottles back and closed the cupboard doors then moved the stool back where it was before she rammed her toe into it.

Secreting herself back against the wall, she waited, barely breathing. Was Margaret getting up or just turning over in her sleep?

After what seemed like a lifetime Emma began to breathe easier. There were no other sounds from overhead.

Not wanting to wait another moment, she tiptoed back to bed as quickly as possible, clutching the pills in her hand.

Pushing the button lock, she slowly pulled the door closed, knowing that there would be a noise when the latch popped into place.

Click! The sound reverberated in the hallway, and again she held her breath. She didn't wait to find out if Margaret heard her. She hurried to her bed, hid the pills between the mattresses, and climbed under the covers. With every muscle tensed, she listened for any sign that Margaret had heard her. Her nerves sparked, giving her anxiety; doubt clouded her mind. How would she get the drugs into Margaret's drink? Once she got the drink spiked with the medicine, what was her plan of action? She needed to find her phone so she could grab it and take it with her when she left. As soon as she got service, she could call for help. The spot where Margaret told her they lost cell phone service was only a few miles down the road.

She had to believe she could do it. She had to. Escape was her only choice. No one knew where she was or what was going on.

Trying to fall asleep, she replayed over and over in her mind exactly how she was going to proceed with her plan.

It had to work, she thought again.

The hope of getting back to Seattle, talking to Landon again, and having normalcy return to her life and to her future gave her the courage she needed to not give up.

9

"GOOD MORNING, MY DEAR." MARGARET entered the room with a smile on her face. She went straight to the window and opened the curtains, letting a flood of sunlight into the room. "It's a beautiful day. The sun makes the snow sparkle like diamonds. I want you to come downstairs and have breakfast with me."

Emma's natural instinct was to refuse, but she knew she would get much further with cooperation than with resistance.

"Thank you," she said, sitting up. She still felt a little achy and nauseous, but this morning it wasn't bad.

She sat up in bed, waiting for Margaret to tell her what to do next, not daring to even blink without permission.

"Well? What are you waiting for?"

"Oh, um, nothing. I'm ready."

As they descended the stairs, Emma remained behind Margaret, feeling nervous and vulnerable. Margaret's emotional instability kept her on guard. She never knew what would trigger the woman's next freak out.

They entered the kitchen, and Margaret motioned for her to sit.

"Scrambled eggs and toast okay?"

Emma nodded.

"Jonathan loved scrambled eggs with cheese sprinkled on top. It was the first thing I ever taught him to make." She cracked eggs into a bowl and whisked in some milk. "He was such a joy. Even though I only had one child, I certainly was blessed to have one who was so wonderful."

Listening to her go on and on about Jonathan's stellar qualities made Emma nauseated. It seemed as though the more Margaret sang his praises, the more Emma wondered if their Jonathans were the same person. Jonathan never cooked scrambled eggs for her once in their marriage. He expected to be waited on hand and foot and never lifted a finger to help around the house. He never did yard work but hired a crew to keep it manicured to his specifications. He was a brilliant doctor, handsome and charming, and he knew it.

If Emma told Margaret how much he used to complain about his mother, she wouldn't believe her. Every time Margaret called, he went like a scared puppy, yet when he got home, he would grumble and complain about his mother being so demanding and needy. Their relationship puzzled Emma; Margaret's perceptions and reality didn't seem to match.

She nodded and smiled at Margaret's memories and stories, but inwardly she prayed constantly for deliverance.

Scraping eggs onto two plates, Margaret brought the food to the table.

"It's so wonderful to have someone to talk to, someone who understands, someone who feels the way I do. You have no idea how much I've needed this."

They both took a bite of their eggs, and Emma couldn't help the "mmm" that escaped her lips.

Margaret smiled. "I knew you'd like them."

Emma felt safe eating the eggs because hers and Margaret's came out of the same pan. She couldn't remember food ever tasting so good.

"That was delicious, thank you." She picked up her plate and took it to the sink. "Would you like me to do the dishes?" she asked Margaret.

"Isn't that thoughtful of you." Margaret smiled with satisfaction. Her smile faded slightly, and she looked over Emma's head at the cupboard above the fridge.

Emma's heart stopped beating. Had Emma forgotten something? Was there something out of place that gave away the fact that she'd been out of her room during the night?

She glanced to where Margaret was looking and couldn't detect anything out of place. She prayed silently for help.

Then she noticed Margaret's coffee cup was empty.

"Would you like some more coffee?"

Lost in concentration it took Margaret a couple of seconds to respond. Then, like she'd snapped out of a trance, she looked at Emma and said, "Yes, thank you."

Hoping she'd diverted the woman's attention away from whatever caught her eye, Emma filled her cup with the realization that she'd found the way to administer the medication to Margaret. Tomorrow, if things played out the same, she would slip the pills into her coffee.

Margaret sipped her coffee while Emma rinsed off the dishes and put them in the dishwasher. She wiped off the counter and put away the eggs, milk, and bread.

"Instead of spending the day in your room, perhaps you'd like to join me in the living room. I brought some home movies with me you might enjoy watching."

Thinking it might give some insight into the family, Emma readily accepted her invitation.

Her feet were freezing by this time, and she sat on the couch in the warmth of the sunshine. A glimmer of hope filled her chest. More than anything she wished Margaret would just see that she didn't need to hold Emma hostage to have a relationship with her, but Margaret didn't want just a normal relationship. She wanted constant, codependent attention, the kind of devotion and companionship that came from a poodle.

"Jonathan was such a cute baby. You know, he slept through the night at one week and never woke up at night again, except when he got sick occasionally. He was just so smart at such an early age. It was that way when he learned to walk. Just pulled himself up to the couch and took off walking. He rarely fell. And when he got potty trained, he never really had any accidents."

Emma smiled at her mother-in-law, trying to show she actually cared, but Jonathan's perfect infancy and childhood didn't particularly add up to the adult he'd become.

"Here we go, dear," Margaret said. She sat down on the couch with Emma and pushed play. The video recording of the home movie started, and on the screen footage of a much younger and quite beautiful Margaret in a hospital bed came on. In her arms was an infant, her newborn son, Jonathan.

"Look how beautiful he was, all that blond hair." Margaret put her hands on her chest and sighed. "Seeing this . . . it seems like yesterday."

Emma had to admit, the newborn Jonathan was about as cute as a baby could get. His round face, full head of blond hair and his big eyes melted her heart. Is that how one of their children would have looked?

Jonathan's father had taken most of the footage, but Margaret took the camera several times and got some video of Charles snuggling with his son. It was precious to see, and Emma's heart was touched by the love displayed on the screen. Margaret was touched as well and sniffed into her handkerchief.

Emma began to see that even though Margaret was controlling, manipulative, and emotionally unstable, she was also painfully lonely. At one moment in her life she was surrounded by love and joy and purpose. But that was gone. Margaret was hopeless and alone. Emma realized she would probably be a little whacked out too if she were in such disparate circumstances.

Next came Jonathan's first birthday party. His cake was shaped like Superman. Apparently he had a huge obsession with Superman because the next two Halloweens showed him wearing a Superman costume with a Superman emblem on the Halloween bucket in his hand. Emma couldn't believe how cute he was.

Footage of Christmas celebrations and a large brightly lit tree followed, and there in front of all the presents was Jonathan, dressed in little Superman pajamas. In front of him was a huge stuffed bear, and his little arms were wrapped around its neck.

"Wow." Emma couldn't hold it in any longer. "He really was adorable."

Margaret smiled at her, her expression reflecting normalcy and the joy of a proud mom. It wasn't enough to make Emma forgive her for the terror she'd caused and for practically scalping her, but she began to think that maybe they could work things out.

"We tried to have more children," Margaret said. "We went through test after test to find out why we couldn't have more children."

Emma opened her mouth to ask what had happened, but she didn't need to ask. Margaret continued talking.

"For years I took pills, went through tests, did all sorts of awful procedures to find out why I couldn't conceive. I became quite an expert on all of it. I worked for a prominent fertility doctor for years, learned everything I could, hoping to discover something that would help me."

The woman's persona began to change as the unpleasant memory distorted her features into a pained expression that slowly transformed into anger.

"My husband wouldn't consider adoption. I liked the idea of adopting because I wanted a daughter desperately. But he wouldn't hear of it." Margaret stared at the corner of the ceiling, vacant and cold. "He only wanted a child that was biologically his. He felt that if we were supposed to have more children then it would happen. I got pregnant twice after that but miscarried both times. The depression consumed me. I spent time in the psych ward, but it didn't really help. No pill or therapy can change the fact that my babies died. All of them."

With an aching heart, Emma began to see the level of pain the woman was in. Her loneliness and anguish at losing every close family member had made her irrationally desperate.

"The worst part is that I knew Charles wasn't faithful to me. It wasn't easy, but I knew my place and accepted it."

Margaret didn't look at her when she spoke. Her eyes were fixed on a distant spot as she recalled the painful memories.

Emma wasn't sure what Margaret wanted from her. Seeing this raw, vulnerable side of her mother-in-law created a turmoil of conflicting emotions. Emma's heart went out to the woman, yet her mind kept her on guard.

"I don't know what—some gut instinct inside me, I guess—caused me to suspect he had fathered another child, perhaps even children. I tried to ignore the thoughts, but they ate me alive. Finally, after he returned from a week-long medical conference in Geneva, I confronted him. I'd learned from a colleague who had attended the same conference that Charles had had a woman staying with him. It was probably wrong of me to have someone spy on my husband, but I just had to know."

Emma wasn't surprised to learn of Charles's infidelity, but the thought that he had other children was a bit of a shock.

"I've never seen him so angry. He told me it was none of my business, what he did when he was away. Who was I to question him? I regretted bringing it up because things changed between us. He never forgave me."

"I'm so sorry," Emma said softly, wishing she had something better to offer.

"I lived in a very dark place for several years. The only thing that forced me to keep going was my son. I knew he would grow up fast. And I clung to the hope that one day I would have grandchildren. But," she paused, looking directly at Emma, "that never happened." Her soft voice, almost a whisper, as she spoke those last words, sent a chill through Emma's bones.

"Margaret . . . ," Emma said, then swallowed, fear closing off her throat. "I wanted children. I was ready to start a family. But Jona—"

"The reasons don't really matter anymore now, do they?" Margaret spoke to her without emotion in her voice. "He's gone. All you have left is your obligation to honor him and his memory."

Emma didn't let her reaction show, but she wondered how Margaret concluded that she had an obligation to Jonathan. He'd been difficult and demanding as a husband. He'd been unfaithful and had not wanted to have children. Once she learned about his infidelity, Emma had decided maybe it was better they didn't have children. She had thought, more than once, about getting divorced. He seemed like a different man from the one she married. She thought she knew him so well, and before they'd gotten married, they'd talked about all the important issues a couple should talk about. He'd said everything she'd wanted to hear; she was convinced he was going to be a wonderful and caring husband and father. Instead he'd turned out to be selfish and controlling.

"And that brings me to the special news I have wanted to share with you. I think we have reached a point in our situation where you are ready to hear it."

Emma gave the woman a level stare. There was something inside Emma that warned her to be prepared for the worst.

"I have to say that even though it will come as a shock to you, I am certain the news will thrill you."

The level of concern inside Emma began to build, like an impending geyser eruption. What was this woman up to?

"After Jonathan's death I hired a private investigator. I wanted an explanation and answers, and I got them. It doesn't please me to say that Jonathan had been with a woman that night. The investigator discovered that this woman was someone who had been in his life for several months. I guess she showed up in the emergency room one night when he was working. She'd been beaten up pretty bad. I'm sure you don't want to hear this, but the fact is they developed a relationship."

Disgust filled Emma until she felt like she would explode with a sudden burst of anger. Even though she knew of his indiscretions, somehow hearing the details made it more painful and forced her to relive her past pain.

Margaret continued to provide unwanted details, which Emma tried to block. But all of her defenses were rendered useless when Margaret said the words, "She's carrying my grandchild."

Emma's mouth dropped open in disbelief.

"Yes, by the time we found her, she had discovered she was pregnant and that the baby is Jonathan's." Margaret clasped her hands together and said with a laugh, "Isn't it wonderful?"

Wonderful? Was she serious?

The woman kept talking, but Emma felt nauseated, sickened by Jonathan's dirty secrets. This was the thanks she got for trying to be a dutiful, loving wife? How could Margaret even be positive it was Jonathan's? Jonathan died the end of May, not quite eight months ago. It was possible, but would a woman like that even know for sure who the father was?

"Of course, we did a paternity test to make sure, and there is no doubt. It's my grandchild. Because of my age, I can't adopt the child, but you . . ."

Margaret's voice faded in and out, like someone was turning the volume up and down on the conversation. A word, here and there, penetrated the fog in her brain.

"Adopt . . . everything you need . . . family . . ."

Was Margaret actually telling her that she had convinced the woman to give up the baby for adoption and that she'd arranged to have Emma adopt the baby?

"No . . . I won't . . ." Emma tried to voice her opposition, but her weakened condition combined with the sheer madness of what Margaret was suggesting proved too much for her. More words formed, but she had no strength to speak. She was losing; there was no fight left in her.

* * *

"Emma." Margaret's voice came through the darkness. Emma's first thought was to run and hide from the woman. In her dreamlike state, it seemed perfectly logical, but as Margaret's voice persisted, Emma's grasp on reality tightened and she realized it was impossible. There was nowhere to hide from the woman or her insanity.

"Let's get you upstairs so you can rest properly," Margaret said. "I know this has all come as a shock to you, so it probably would be good just to relax and let it all soak in."

Holding back her urge to completely freak out, Emma eyed Margaret suspiciously, feeling like a cornered cat, ready to pounce.

"I will warm up some soup and bring it to you."

Emma clutched her nightgown to her throat and shrank back, trusting nothing Margaret had to say. Her shoulder hurt again. Another injection.

"Everything is okay," Margaret said, her tone dripping with saccharine sweetness. "You'll feel better after some food and rest. Go on now."

Emma couldn't think clearly. Mentally and physically she felt completely broken. Obeying Margaret's command she headed for the stairs, ascending slowly, one by one.

Just when she had actually found some insight and understanding into Margaret's pain, Margaret dropped an atomic sized piece of her plan that exploded inside like a bomb.

Emma could barely put one foot in front of the other. Her emotions and thoughts shot back and forth across her brain, colliding wildly, causing pain and confusion and sheer terror.

Margaret could not seriously think Emma would go through with this, that she would actually adopt Jonathan's love child with another woman.

Her head pounded with the enormity of Margaret's convoluted plan and irrational thinking. She had to get out of there. Now!

She fell against the wall of the hallway leading to her bedroom and drew in several ragged breaths, trying desperately not to cry until she got to her room.

She couldn't believe that just a few minutes ago she'd begun to feel sorry for Margaret. It was obvious that the woman had probably suffered from postpartum depression or some sort of hormonal imbalances on top of her other issues. Not having a devoted husband hadn't helped. Her guess was that the crazier Margaret got, the more he probably withdrew from her, causing her to be more clingy, demanding, and dependent.

Gaining an understanding of Margaret's state of mind helped her clearly see what she was dealing with, but Emma didn't feel sorry for the woman any longer. She couldn't. Any compassion she felt would create weakness. She had to stay strong.

The cold of her room forced her under the covers, and she curled up in a ball to get warm again. Closing her eyes she offered a prayer, even praying for Margaret. She understood now that the woman was in pain and unstable, and she begged Heavenly Father to help Margaret see how irrationally she was behaving.

It would be wise to sleep with one eye open. She knew Margaret was capable of anything and desperate enough to do whatever it took to make things happen the way she wanted them too.

As she finally began to warm up, she felt sleep overtake her. With her hunger pains gone, her stomach knotted with worry. A constant prayer ran through her mind: a prayer for help, for strength, and for deliverance from this nightmare.

10

"Do you see her?" Jess asked.

Cassie shook her head. "I hope she didn't change her mind. We have to get that report."

Jess prayed that Melissa would have the courage she needed to help them. Without her they wouldn't be able to recruit the help of the police in finding Emma; otherwise they would be storming up the mountain to bang on the door of every cabin up there.

"Once we meet up with Melissa, we'd better call Landon. If we get the police to help us, we'll find her. I know we will."

"I do too," Cassie said, looking over Jess's shoulder. "I think I see her."

Cass waved her hand, and Jess turned around to see the young receptionist walking through the food court of the mall toward them, wearing sunglasses and a trench coat.

As she hurried their direction, Melissa kept looking side to side then glancing behind her. Her action made her look so suspicious Jess was surprised someone hadn't alerted the authorities and reported her as a possible terrorist or drug dealer.

"Hi," Cassie said enthusiastically.

Melissa shushed her and darted to a darkened corner of the food court covered by indoor houseplants and a half wall.

Cassie and Jess exchanged glances then shrugged and sat down.

"Thank you for meeting us," Jess said.

"I think I'm being followed," Melissa said, sliding low in her seat and covering her face with her hand.

Cassie and Jess looked back across the food court. A woman with three small children, several high school–aged girls, and an elderly couple completed the rest of the occupants of the food court. Their gazes met. Cassie rolled her eyes, and Jess nearly started laughing.

"I think you're safe," Jess told her, flashing a warning look at Cassie. The girl had gone out on a limb for them, and she didn't want to make her feel like they didn't appreciate it.

Melissa reached into her oversized purse and pulled out a manila folder and slid it across the table to them.

"That should be everything you need to prove that Margaret Lowell is completely insane. The doctor gave her a diagnosis but wanted further mental assessments done to delve deeper into her psyche because her case is so extreme."

"Does it say all that in the report?" Cassie asked.

Melissa nodded.

"This is going to help so much. We don't know how to thank you," Jess said.

"Normally I wouldn't be willing to risk my job for something like this, but I believe your friend is in a lot of danger. I can't explain it, but Margaret Lowell is seriously disturbed. Every employee who ever worked with her commented on how horribly she treated them. Sometimes it was just verbal put-downs and broad generalizations, but sometimes she was violent and cruel. Most of them were scared of her, and that includes the men."

"She's an old lady, for crying out loud," Cassie said.

"Who is freakishly strong and has a horrible temper. You two better be careful if you get close to her." Melissa peeked over the half wall through the plants. "I need to get going. Please, keep my name out of this."

"We will. The last thing we want is for you to get into trouble," Jess assured her.

"Good luck." Melissa pulled the collar of her trench coat up and held her purse close to her chest. She left their table and exited a different way than she came.

"I bet the doctors could pin a few mental disorders on that chick," Cassie said.

"Cassie!" Jess reprimanded.

"Sorry, I'm just saying, someone's a tad bit delusional and paranoid."

"She helped us when no one else would."

"You're right, but that girl needs some therapy. She's going to have a nervous breakdown."

Jess opened the file and looked down at the report in front of her. She scanned to find something about the diagnosis and the doctor's recommendation.

Cassie joined her, and at the exact same time, they located the information they were looking for.

"Obsessive-compulsive with greater emphasis on the narcissistic personality disorder," Jess read out loud.

"I don't know what that means, but it sounds like a bad combination."

"Let's get to the police station. Now!"

"Okay. Don't you get crazy on me," Cassie said.

"I don't think you saw this part." Jess pointed to a line at the bottom of the report where there were several questions with boxes next to them.

One question read, "Is patient a danger to themselves?"

The box was checked, *Possibly*.

The next question read, "Is patient a danger to others?"

The box was checked, *Yes*.

"Cassie, this is worse than we thought. Let's go!"

* * *

A loud crash and the sound of glass shattering woke Emma with a start.

"Help! Please, help me!" Margaret's weak and pain-filled voice called from across the hallway.

"What in the world?" Emma threw off the covers and sat up quickly, nearly toppling out of bed. It took several seconds to clear the sleep from her mind. When she stepped on the icy cold floor, she became completely awake.

"Help!" Margaret's voice came again but was weaker.

Emma threw the door of her room open, and she raced across the hall. Margaret's bedroom door was open, and a small nightlight near Margaret's bed guided her toward her mother-in-law.

She charged into the room but searing pain suddenly shot up from the soles of her feet as she stepped on sharp objects that sliced into her flesh.

She cried out as she froze, the objects digging deeper into her feet. Seeing the outline of the bed within reach, she fell forward, hoping to make it onto the mattress.

"What are you doing?" Margaret yelled at her.

"My feet!" she screamed, the pain sending a wave of nausea over her.

Margaret exited the bed on the opposite side.

"Help!" Emma screamed.

Margaret made her way to the light switch by the door and flipped it on.

The shattered remnants of the antique hurricane lamp from Margaret's nightstand lay on the floor in puddles of blood.

Swallowing the bile that rose in her throat at the sight of the blood, Emma looked down at her feet and saw multiple shards of glass wedged deeply in the flesh.

She tried to pull out one of the smaller pieces, but the room suddenly began to spin and nausea rose inside of her.

"I think I'm going to be sick," she said, just before she threw up.

* * *

"This is not a certified copy of the report," the police officer said. "I don't think it will hold up in court."

"Right now we don't care about that," Cassie said. "All we care about is if it's enough to get some help from this police department. Time is of the essence!"

"Give me just a minute." He left his desk carrying the report in front of him.

Cassie waited until he was out of earshot before she threw her hands up and growled. "Could he be any slower? I swear I'm going to freak out, and I'm talking Mount Vesuvius–sized here."

"Shh, here he comes." The detective returned with another man behind him.

"Ladies, this is Detective Bradley."

They both greeted him.

"Detective Bradley is being assigned to your case. I'm going to turn things over to him. I'm sure he has some questions for you."

Detective Bradley gave them a nod and took a chair.

"So, I need just a little detail and background, and we can get started."

"We needed to get started yesterday!" Cassie exclaimed.

"Miss, I realize you're worried about your friend, but if you can just take a minute to bring me up to speed with the events that took place prior to her disappearance and any information you might feel is helpful, we will be able to construct a plan of action."

Cassie groaned.

"I've got this," Jess said, patting her friend on the shoulder. "Go get a drink or something, and I'll fill Detective Bradley in on everything."

Cassie shoved her chair back and stood. "Okay, but don't forget the conversation we had with Margaret's sister." She turned to walk away. "Oh, and the nurse at the hospital who was terrified of the woman. And—"

"I won't forget anything," Jess assured her.

Detective Bradley and Jess watched Cassie leave then Jess cleared her throat and said, "I'm sorry. We're both very tired and very worried. Cassie is an extremely nice person, she's just frustrated."

"I understand, ma'am. If you'll start at the beginning . . ."

* * *

As Emma attempted to open her eyes, blinding light greeted her as well as a painful throbbing in her feet.

"Ow," she breathed out the word then bit her lip to keep from crying out again. Tears filled her eyes.

"Some of those cuts were pretty bad," Margaret spoke, causing Emma to flinch. She didn't know the woman was in her room.

"Why didn't you warn me?"

Margaret just looked at her then began putting away first aid supplies.

Emma didn't like the expression on the woman's face. There was no sympathy or concern for Emma's pain. Instead, it looked like there was satisfaction in her eyes.

"Margaret," she spoke with firmness, "why didn't you warn me?"

The woman said nothing.

"You were calling for help. What did you need?"

A smile grew on the woman's face. "I needed you to do exactly what you did."

"Come into your room and step on glass?"

Margaret nodded.

Rage, like a grenade, exploded inside of her. "What! You wanted me to slice my feet to shreds?" She struggled to sit up; she couldn't lie there and listen to this. Her right foot smacked against the footboard sending a whole new wave of pain washing over her.

Hot tears filled her eyes and spilled onto her cheeks. She pounded the bed with her fists, her shoulder exploding in pain, indicating that Margaret had given her another injection. Emma felt like she was slipping deeper and deeper into a dark, bottomless pit. She made no sound but couldn't stop the tears that fell.

Her emotions did nothing to trigger sympathy from Margaret.

"You're insane!" Emma said, using the sheet to wipe her face. She pushed on her temples as her head began to throb. Margaret had a self-serving agenda, and no matter what the cost, she was going to have things her way.

"Why? Why did you do this to me?"

"Hmph," Margaret responded, "because I couldn't trust you."

Emma shook her head as tears stung her eyes. The hopelessness of her situation became completely clear to her.

"You honestly didn't think I'd notice that you stole meds from me."

An electrifying jolt tore through Emma, but she fought to hide her reaction, not wanting to give Margaret the satisfaction that she had Emma in her control.

"If I'm to get any sleep, I need to know you won't be up at night prowling around the house. I think we both agree that I took care of the problem. Now," she said, stepping closer to Emma, a pair of scissors in her hand, "where are the pills you took?"

Emma still couldn't believe the woman had discovered her. All hope vanished. Any chance of escape was gone.

"Emma," Margaret held the scissors out at a threatening angle, "don't force me to hurt you again."

"Under the mattress," Emma said, pointing to the spot where she'd tucked the pills away.

"I had a dog that had to learn everything the hard way," Margaret said. "No matter how many times I told him to stay, he disobeyed. Do you know what happened to him?"

Emma winced in pain but turned her head slightly toward the woman so Margaret would know she was listening.

"He died. It was his own fault. He constantly disobeyed me."

Emma understood clearly what she was saying. And after the broken glass, she believed her.

"I didn't want it to be this way. I wanted us to share this time together. Especially now that I've shared with you the special journey we have ahead of us." Her eyes narrowed and anger filled her expression. "But you are ruining everything."

The fact that the woman seriously expected Emma to go along with her ridiculous plan was evidence enough of Margaret's state of mind.

"Margaret, please, you can't think—"

"Silence!"

Feeling like Margaret had just slapped her across the face, Emma looked at the woman, stunned and frightened.

"I have something for you to sign," Margaret said, taking a handful of papers off the nightstand. She shoved a pen into Emma's hand and slammed the papers onto Emma's stomach, causing Emma to cry out from the pain of the blow.

"I will never—"

"Oh yes, you will. I'm choosing to 'let' you sign, rather than forcing you to sign, but if I need to do it the other way, I will."

Emma didn't move. She was frantically trying to figure out how to handle the situation, but Margaret held all the power and had proved that she would stop at nothing to get her way.

"Sign the paper, Emma."

Emma swallowed hard and tears filled her eyes. She looked down at the document on her lap and prayed for help, for a miracle.

"Sign the paper!" Margaret yelled.

Emma jumped and her tears fell. She didn't see an option. She couldn't endure much more. Surely no court would find the document binding under these circumstances.

With a trembling hand she signed the paper, then let the pen fall, her body collapsing in defeat.

"Do not leave this room tonight," Margaret said through gritted teeth, snatching the paper from her. "Do you understand?"

Emma nodded.

"Tomorrow we will talk about the next step. You will learn, Emma, that I am not the bad guy. I am giving you everything . . . financial security and a greater purpose in life."

It was all Emma could do not to lash out, somehow attack her captor, but she was broken, completely drained. The fight was gone.

Margaret left the room, taking the first aid supplies with her.

The pain in Emma's feet, coupled with the pain in her heart was too much. Her body shook with the sobs that overtook her.

* * *

Emma's sleep was interrupted by nightmares and moments of terror that jarred her awake. Immediately when her eyes opened, she began crying. Her situation was more than she could bear. She wondered how long this was going to go on and if there was any chance of them being discovered, any chance anyone would find them.

Her chest constricted with fear as she realized that if, even as a member of the family, she had known nothing of the cabin, chances were no one else did either. Her only hope of rescue was herself. She had to escape. But how she was going to do that was another question. Her feet throbbed constantly, reminding her that walking wasn't even an option right now, let alone trudging through the snow.

Her previous plan of drugging Margaret and leaving was still possible, but she would have to be even more careful about acquiring the medicine. She'd learned the hard way that Margaret kept count of the pills in the bottles.

Her final thought before falling back to sleep was that if she was going to die, she would rather have it happen while she was trying to escape than sitting there like a deer in the crosshairs of a gun scope.

* * *

Wrapped in a blanket, Emma sat by the window, looking out at the clear, sun-filled day. Another day came and went, but time had lost meaning and felt like she was suspended in the Twilight Zone. Most of the time the sky was overcast and snow fell, but this morning the bright light from the sun was a welcome change and actually lifted her spirits, somehow giving her a glimpse of hope that maybe something good was going to happen.

At the very corner of the window, she noticed the large structure behind the cabin. The garage. She suspected that it was big enough to store equipment and tools and was even big enough . . . for a snowmobile?

Was it possible?

She remembered the snowmobile clothing in the closet and Margaret's reference to using snowmobiles to get in and out of the cabin in the winter. Was there any chance there were snowmobiles in there?

How could she find out?

"Good morning."

Emma let out a startled cry, clutching the blanket closer around her. Having Margaret enter the room as she was planning her escape gave her a start.

"It's a beautiful day out there," Margaret said.

Emma nodded and cast her gaze back to the view outside the window. A pressure inside her chest and a longing for her life to return to normal and to be with Landon felt like it was being crushed. Tears were near the surface. She'd never experienced an emotional breakdown, but she felt like she was on the verge of completely freaking out. Staying indoors, feeling suffocated and captive, fed her anxiety and challenged her coping mechanisms.

"I brought you some eggs and toast," Margaret said. "And something for the pain in your feet. I need to check the band—"

The woman stepped closer, and Emma leaned away from her, clutching the blanket to her neck.

"You're trembling," Margaret said. She put her hand to Emma's forehead, but Emma flinched, jerking her head back.

Margaret persisted and felt her forehead. "Hmm, you're either burning up or cold and clammy. Oh dear."

Fear, anxiety, and panic began to build like a chemical reaction of nuclear proportions. Emma felt an eruption about to happen. She couldn't stand it any longer.

With a nod of her head, Margaret muttered to herself, "I was afraid of this."

She set the tray down on the bed and left the room. Emma listened as her footsteps descended the stairs and traveled across the floor below. A few moments later the footsteps returned, and Margaret came back into the room.

Watching the woman's every move, Emma knew something bad was about to happen. Her survival instincts kicked in, and a surge of adrenalin coursed through her veins.

"Emma, everything is okay," Margaret spoke in a calming voice. "I think you're having an allergic reaction to one of the medications. I'm going to give you something to help with the side effects."

Emma shook her head and pushed hersef back, away from the approaching madwoman.

"You're going to be fine, dear. I know this must be upsetting for you, but just trust me. It's all for your own good."

How in the world was it for her good? Emma wanted to scream at the woman. In what twisted and horrible existence was what she was doing acceptable?

"Just stay calm. I can help you."

Her slow approach gave Emma a chance to prepare for an attack. She'd already decided she would rather die trying to escape than remain a prisoner to this mad woman. She didn't allow her expression to belie her intentions.

"Trust me, Emma. You have so much to gain if you will."

Margaret stood with one hand behind her back. Emma didn't have to see what was behind her to know it wasn't good.

Like a cornered animal, Emma waited for her to make a move.

"Good," Margaret said, "just breathe and stay calm. Everything is going to be—"

From behind her back Margaret wielded a syringe, which she plunged toward Emma. But this time Emma was ready. She dodged the needle and caught Margaret off-guard. With unexpected strength she grabbed the woman's hand and twisted it behind her back forcing her to drop the syringe.

Margaret cried out in surprise and pain, but Emma was deaf to her pleas. She kept hold of Margaret's arm and reached down for the syringe. When she raised back up, Margaret took a swing at her with her other arm, knocking Emma on the side of the head.

Stunned briefly but still keeping her grip, Emma didn't waste another second. Making a direct hit to Margaret's arm, she jammed the needle into the woman's shoulder muscle and shot the contents into her.

Margaret screamed and recoiled clutching her shoulder. "You don't know what you've done!"

"I'm giving you a taste of your own medicine!" Emma yelled back at her. "It's over, Margaret! I'm done with this madness. You're insane! I won't let you control or destroy my life!"

Margaret began to sob, as her body grew limp on the floor. "I had such wonderful plans. You had so much to gain, and you're ruining everything. What about the baby?"

"Your son was a horrible husband, and I would rather die than raise his child from another woman!" Emma yelled at her.

"It's too late, you've already signed the papers, and I've hidden them." Margaret's voice became slurred.

"That won't matter after people find out what you've done to me. It's over, Margaret! It's over!"

Emma looked around for something to use to tie up Margaret. She limped to the chest of drawers and opened each one, finding a pair of sweat pants, a T-shirt, and several pair of socks.

"My grandbaby," Margaret cried. "My sweet, sweet grandbaby."

"It might be your grandbaby, but it will never be my child."

"You don't understand," Margaret said.

"What don't I understand?"

"The medicine I've been giving you . . ."

Emma stopped and looked at Margaret, fear clutching her heart.

"What about the medicine?" she demanded.

Margaret looked away and began to chuckle.

"Margaret! What about the medicine?"

"I knew you'd struggle with the adoption, so . . ."

Emma waited for her to continue, her brain trying to piece together events from the last few days to help her figure out what Margaret was about to say.

Margaret closed her eyes and didn't answer.

"Margaret! Tell me what you've done!"

With eyes still shut and a smile on her face, Margaret remained silent.

"I need to know!" Emma said, unable to hide the desperation in her plea.

"Those injections have triggered an early menopause. It's too late, Emma."

"What do you mean, it's too late?"

Margaret's words came slurred and heavy. "You'll never have children of your own."

"You're lying!" Emma yelled as Margaret's body went limp. "Tell me you're lying!"

Margaret didn't answer.

"No! Margaret, no!"

Emma painfully made her way to the old woman and fell to her knees. She shook Margaret's shoulders trying to wake her, but the woman was completely unconscious.

Grief overtook her, and Emma collapsed onto the floor. She felt her heart breaking, and the small sliver of life left that Margaret hadn't destroyed drained out into a puddle around her. Slowly, she sank to the floor, adding tears to the puddle.

What would Landon say? They'd talked about starting their family right away. They were both anxious and ready for children. And now that wouldn't happen.

Unable to process the devastating news and the entire situation, Emma felt herself sinking. Her fight was gone. Sobs wracked her body, and she let the dam break free. All her fears, nightmares, and shock of the last few days erupted.

Her mind replayed all the horrors she'd suffered, all the craziness and absurdity of Margaret's reasoning, and the final blow of knowing that Margaret had possibly rendered her barren; it was too much.

Feeling like a shell, she felt the quiet settle in as her sobs grew quiet and her tears stopped. There was nothing left.

She lifted her head to look at Margaret, sleeping peacefully, eerily with both hands on her chest like a corpse in a coffin.

Emma couldn't believe a person was capable of inflicting such mental, emotional, and physical torture on another human. It was impossible to understand, yet Emma still tried. Clearly Margaret suffered from some serious mental issues, probably compounded by the deep pain of her husband's and son's deaths. It had pushed the already unstable woman over the edge.

Whatever reason Margaret had, Emma wasn't about to let her destroy her life. Landon loved her, and he would help her face whatever the future held.

The future. There was so much to look forward to, so much to anticipate.

Emma wanted it all. She wanted to go to the temple with Landon, to have a family, to work together to build a life, to grow old together.

But it wasn't going to happen if she didn't get out of there.

Her fingers balled into a fist. Using the claim that she was going to give her everything, Margaret had nearly taken everything away from Emma. But that was about to change.

She pounded her fist on the floor. No! Margaret was not going to win. Emma was taking her life back!

Weak from hunger, thirst, and the abuse she'd suffered, Emma felt a fire of survival ignite, sending a surge of power and strength to her muscles.

This whole twisted plot of Margaret's was not happening. She was getting out of there, or she would die trying.

It was all she could do to push herself off the floor, but as she moved, she felt stronger and her resolved strengthened.

First thing she had to do was secure Margaret and make sure the woman wouldn't come after her.

Grabbing a pair of tube socks from the drawer, she pulled Margaret's limp arms behind her and used one of the long socks to tie them together at the wrists. She then tied the woman's ankles together.

Margaret cried softly, mumbling about a grandbaby and her family legacy.

Satisfied that Margaret was down for the count, Emma turned back to the drawer and pulled on the sweatpants and T-shirt and put on the other pair of socks.

Hobbling, she left the confines of her room and painfully descended the stairs, feeling the socks moistening with blood from her wounds. Ignoring the pain, she made her way downstairs to the closet and found the boots and outerwear she remembered.

With all the appropriate outerwear, there had to be a snowmobile in that shed. Somehow she knew one would be there, and she could finally escape.

Crying out in pain as she walked, she braced herself for the cold as she stepped outside the back door. The snow was almost to her knees, and it fell inside the boots. But the cold felt good. The crisp air helped clear the fog from her brain and sharpened her senses.

Trudging through the thick snow, she felt like screaming with relief at the top of her lungs. She was finally out of that house, out of that woman's clutches.

"Please, God. Let there be some way for me to escape inside that shed."

The plea continued looping through her mind as she made her way to the door. A padlock hung from the door latch, taunting her. The small object was her only obstacle to possible freedom.

She looked around for a tool or pipe to use to break the lock, but everything was covered in snow.

If she only knew where Margaret had put her clothes, she could find the keys. Maybe there was a key to the garage on it. If not, there had to be a hammer in the house, or some other tool. She had to go back in and find something. She wasn't going to let this window of opportunity close on her.

Back to the cabin she trudged, each step sending a hot shooting pain through her feet. Cries of agony escaped in visible puffs of air, her tears freezing her cheeks, but nothing was going to stand in her way. This ordeal, this madness and nightmare, was over!

Clamoring inside the back door, she began throwing open cupboards and yanking open drawers inside the kitchen. Finding nothing she then moved to the laundry room. She stopped in her tracks. There on the counter was Margaret's purse.

Not wasting a second, she tore through the contents and gasped when she found her phone and Margaret's.

Finally, things were turning around.

She looked frantically for her clothes but found nothing.

"Please, Father, help me!" She didn't find a hammer, but she found a large screwdriver and a pair of pliers. She also found a long lighter and got another idea. If she were able to get away in a vehicle, she would light the shed on fire. Hopefully someone would see the smoke.

Shielding her eyes from the brightness of the sun reflecting on the glistening snow, Emma followed her previous footsteps back to the shed.

Standing in front of the door, Emma took a moment to check both phones for service, but still no luck. She would continue to check, but for now she had to get inside that shed.

* * *

"Please don't make us stay behind. We'll go crazy," Cassie begged.

"We won't get in the way, we promise," Jess added.

"Listen," Detective Bradley said with measured tones. "We have no way of knowing how dangerous the situation is, and we aren't about to put you both in harm's way. I'm sorry, but you'll have to stay back. I will keep you apprised of the situation as we locate your friend and assess the situation."

"What if we promise to stay out of the way? Please, let us follow you."

Detective Bradley's gaze shifted to Jess.

"Sorry," she shrugged. "I'm with her."

The detective's head dropped back, and he released a sigh that sounded more like a frustrated growl. "We still need to find out where this cabin is and get a search warrant," he explained.

"You'll get it," Cassie said without hesitation. "We've come this far; we can't stop now."

"All right," he held up both hands. "I can't stop you from following us, but you have to give me your word that you will stay back and out of the way."

"We promise!" Cassie exploded. She grabbed Jess's hand. "Come on!"

They raced to Jess's Honda CR-V and climbed in before Detective Bradley could change his mind.

Jess started the vehicle then said, with a tight grip on the steering wheel, "I don't know how to drive in the snow." Her car was all-wheel-drive but that didn't mean she actually went places that required it.

"It will be okay. I'm sure the roads have been plowed by now, and the sun has been out a lot today. We'll be fine. Don't worry."

Cassie's strong conviction gave a boost to Jess's doubts. Cassie was right. They finally had a lead and a general idea of where the cabin could be; they weren't about to let anything stop them, especially a little snow!

"They're pulling out," Cassie exclaimed. "Follow them and stay close. I could see them trying to ditch us."

"I will," Jess said, stomping on the gas. The SUV lurched forward, the tires squealing with the movement.

"Woo-hoo! We're coming, Emma!" Cassie yelled, pumping one arm in the air.

Jess couldn't help but laugh. "I think you missed your calling in life."

"What do you mean?"

"I'm sure you're great at doing real estate, but seriously, I think you could be a private investigator. Do you get this excited to show houses?"

Cassie thought for a minute. "Nope. I do when I get a sale though. Oh look, they're already getting on the freeway. Change lanes so you can exit."

Jess followed her command and deftly changed lanes without cutting off any drivers.

"Good job, Jess!"

Keeping an eye on the patrol car in front of her, Jess narrowed the gap between the two vehicles and kept pace with them. She wasn't about to let them get away.

She glanced sideways at Cassie, who was busy on her phone, and thought about how bizarre the events of the last few days had been and marveled that she was with Cassie and they were trying to find Emma. Not in a million years could she have dreamed of the situation they were in.

She just prayed they would find Emma in time.

"Have you ever met Margaret Lowell?" Emma asked Cassie.

"Nope. I didn't know Emma when Jonathan died. You?"

"I saw her at the viewing and funeral but never spoke to her. She looked like a classy, rich lady; she came off a little snobbish, but I wouldn't guess her to be crazy."

"People snap, especially if they have mental issues, which we know she clearly has. I just read online about a guy who had dementia and thought his wife was a secret spy and she was trying to poison him. When she tried to give him his heart medicine, he stabbed and killed her with a pair of scissors, out of self-defense. People snap, especially when they are backed into a corner."

Jess tried to push away the panic that rose up inside of her as she imagined what could possibly be happening with Emma. Hopefully it was all a big misunderstanding and Emma was fine but didn't have phone service to let them know she was okay.

The cell phone in her shirt pocket vibrated, indicating an incoming call.

Just as she'd hoped, it was Landon.

"Hi, Landon, how are—"

"I'm almost there, we land in less than an hour."

"You're calling from the plane?"

"Yes, this has been the longest flight of my life! What's going on there? Any news?"

"Didn't you get my text? We're on our way to the cabin right now."

"You and Cassie? I'm not sure that's—"

"We aren't alone. We're following two police cars. With the information we got from Margaret's sister, they think we can locate the cabin. I guess there has been a lot of snow though, so getting to it might be another story. They are trying to contact the sheriff's office to find out if they have access to snowmobiles."

"I'm so relieved you've finally been able to get the authorities involved."

"Once we got the report confirming that Margaret is unstable and dangerous, they kicked into action."

"Can you text me the directions so I can come as soon as I land?"

"Sure, but you don't have a car at the airport."

"I have a friend at work picking me up. He drives a Jeep, so we'll just head to where you guys are when I arrive."

"Okay, we'll give you detailed directions. I'm glad you're almost here. I can't imagine how hard this has been."

"It's been the worst. I can't imagine what Emma is going through right now. I keep telling myself there has to be a logical explanation for what's happening, but I can't find one. She wouldn't just take off like this without letting me know, or one of you."

"That's how we feel."

"I'll be in touch as soon as we land. Keep me posted. And Jess?"

"Yes?" She signaled to change lanes.

"Thank you both." There was a catch in his voice.

"You're welcome. Don't worry, Landon. We'll find her."

Jess ended the call and slid her phone into her pocket.

"He's worried sick, isn't he?" Cassie asked.

"Yes, the poor man is going crazy trying to get here. Can you imagine how long that flight must have felt for him?"

Cassie shook her head. They rode in silence for a moment then Cassie started to chuckle.

"What?" Jess couldn't imagine what Cassie found funny.

"What if we get there and Emma and Margaret are just chillin' in the cabin, you know, drinking hot chocolate and watching old movies, spending some quality mother-in-law/daughter-in-law time together?"

Jess looked at her then quickly back at the road.

Cassie burst out laughing. "I said, 'what if.' I just pictured us all bursting into the cabin and surprising them, and they're both on the couch in Snuggies, watching TV."

"You know, I hope that's exactly what we do find."

* * *

The searing pain on the bottom of her feet forced Emma to stop and take some deep breaths. She'd never had a strong stomach around blood and injuries, and the thought of the snow boots filling up with the blood from her wounds made her lightheaded and nauseated.

"Help me, Father," she said out loud. "Help me do this!"

With renewed strength, she inserted the long nose of the screwdriver into the hooked neck of the lock. Then with all the effort she could muster, she yanked trying to free the mechanism that held it tight. Again and again she pulled and twisted and fought with the strength of the steel lock. No amount of prying or pounding would release it.

She stepped back, her breath creating puffs of steam in the cold, and surveyed the structure. All the windows were high up and small. Even if she broke one, there was no way she could climb inside.

She remembered the lighter and wondered if she could burn down the door, at least the area around the latch. Would it work? She could throw snow on it to keep it from getting out of control.

Then she realized that, after all the medication and mind games Margaret had used on her, she wasn't sure her thoughts even made sense. She couldn't come up with any other idea. She also knew she couldn't waste any time wondering. She was just going to go for it.

It took several tries before the wood finally caught fire but soon the door had a small flicker of a flame lapping at the grains of dry wood.

So far so good. The flames continued to grow, and she realized this possibly could work.

The warmth from the fire felt good. Her cheeks and nose were ice cold.

Flames grew stronger and spread, and she began to worry that the whole door was going to go up. She began throwing handfuls of snow onto the fire to prevent it from consuming too much wood.

Smoke began to sting her eyes and make her cough.

Panic began to rise in her chest. It was getting too big, too fast!

Faster and faster she flung snow at the door, but the flames were getting so hot and the smoke so thick she couldn't get close enough or throw enough snow to slow it down.

If there were snowmobiles inside, she was about to burn them down!

Feeling helpless she kept heaving snow but knew it was pointless. The fire was growing out of control.

Tears began to fall onto her cheeks as she realized this was her chance to escape and she had no way of leaving. She couldn't get inside the garage. She had to make something happen.

The heat of the fire was too much, and she retreated, tears still falling and fear inside of her rising.

Was there a solution she wasn't seeing? Was there a different way down the mountain?

She recalled a large storage closet in the laundry room. Was there something in there she could use? Snowshoes? A sled?

She headed back to the house and was almost inside when a foreign sound suddenly captured her attention.

A crackling and hiss filled the air then a loud pop. The strong odor of smoke filled her nostrils.

She turned and couldn't believe her eyes.

11

THE FRONT HALF OF THE shed was completely engulfed in flames. Black smoke billowed through the trees, melting the snow on the branches above, which did little to curb the flame's appetite.

That was it. It didn't matter what was in the shed. She was leaving. Someone would have to see the smoke and come to find out what was burning. She would meet them as they came up the road.

Her muscles burned, her feet screamed in pain, but she didn't care. Adrenalin and the joy of knowing she was free filled her with energy and determination. She remembered the phone in her pocket. If she got far enough down the road, she might get service, then she could call for help. This was going to work. It just had to.

Holding a phone in each hand, she checked for service every few steps.

"Come on," she said, hoping bars would appear at her urging.

With labored, pain-filled steps, she trudged through the deep snow. She approached the spot where Landon's car had slid off the road. Just the site of his car caused her heart to clench so hard in her chest it made her groan in agony. What was he thinking right now? Certainly he had to be overcome with worry that he'd had no contact in . . . how many days? She'd lost track. She had no idea what day it was or how long she'd been held captive.

Suddenly she was aware of a roaring behind her. She turned to see the flames climbing high above the roof of the shed in the distance. The intensity of the blaze alarmed her. What had she done?

Another pop sounded and then an ear-shattering *BOOM* shook the ground and sent debris flying. The trees surrounding the shed became engulfed in the flames, and, to her horror, the back corner of the porch on the main cabin.

"Oh no! No!" She stood, frozen with fear. Margaret was inside; completely unaware of what was going on. If the house went up as fast as the shed . . .

"What have I done!" she screamed. She had no time to lose. It didn't matter that Margaret was crazy and had tortured her. She couldn't let the woman burn to death.

Feeling like she was running in slow motion, Emma fought her way to the cabin, praying that she would get there in time. Her boots were sticky inside with blood, but she ignored them.

The cold air burned her lungs and her muscles screamed as she pushed ahead finally arriving at the front door. Thankfully it was unlocked, and she burst through ignoring the danger inside.

"Margaret, I'm coming!" she yelled as she raced for the stairs, her oversized, heavy boots impeding her progress. She fell, ramming her knee into the edge of a step but didn't stop. She had to get her and Margaret out of there!

The roar of the fire and heavy smell of smoke told her she had minutes before the cabin was consumed.

"Margaret!" she screamed over the inferno and stumbled down the hallway to the bedroom where she found Margaret unconscious on the floor.

Smoke began to seep into the room, and Emma coughed, covering her mouth and nose with her arm. "God, please help me!"

She fell to her knees and shook Margaret, hoping to rouse her, but Margaret just groaned and mumbled then tried to roll away from her.

Emma tried again but got the same response.

Staying low to the ground, Emma reached toward the bed and pulled the comforter off then spread it out next to Margaret. She rolled the woman onto the comforter and began to pull. Luckily the wood floors helped her slide Margaret's body more easily, and soon they were in the hallway.

Black smoke filled the air and stung Emma's eyes. She pulled the neck of her shirt up over her nose so she could breathe, but she was running out of energy.

"Help!" she cried to the heavens as she dragged Margaret's body to the stairs.

Glad they were descending rather than going up the stairs, Emma tried her best to hold Margaret under her arms as they bumped their way down the stairs. The popping and roaring of the flames made her feel like they were sitting on top of a ticking bomb.

Alarmed at how quickly the fire was spreading, she no longer felt the pain in her feet or in her muscles. With every step she was closer to safety, and she was determined to keep them both alive.

With a loud crash, the roof in the hallway caved in with globs of flaming sheetrock and insulation tumbling onto the ground and down the stairs. A burning section of log-pole pine landed on the blanket, starting it on fire.

Emma screamed and, without a second thought, rolled Margaret's body off the comforter and pulled her down the rest of the stairs, leaving the flaming comforter behind.

"How are you so heavy for such a small woman!" Emma yelled at her mother-in-law as she dragged her body across the floor, the cabin collapsing above them with each step they took. Smoke was thick and filling the entire structure, and Emma wheezed for breath as she fought to get them the last few steps to the door and outside to safety.

Spying a fleece throw blanket on the chair by the entrance, she grabbed it and threw it on top of Margaret then took one last heaving step out the front door as the structure above them seemed to completely collapse.

"Margaret, wake up!" Emma screamed, but the woman was completely out. "Please, Father, help us. I can't make it much farther."

Underneath an enormous pine tree twenty yards from the house was some bare ground.

Walking backwards, dragging Margaret through the snow, Emma pushed her strength to the limit. "Almost there," she told herself. "You can do this."

Ducking under the branches, heavily laden with snow, Emma crumbled on top of a bed of pine needles around the base of the tree. She fell back, gasping for air, Margaret's body slumped across her own. They were alive. For now that had to be enough.

Occasional blasts and surges of flames filled her with terror as she watched the cabin get eaten alive by the fire she'd started. The heat of the blaze was almost too much to bear, even from such a distance.

Emma shivered, her body weak and trembling, her breath coming faster. A feeling of nausea overwhelmed her, and she broke out in a cold sweat. She pulled in breaths as quickly as she could to curb the nausea but only made herself lightheaded. Rolling to her side, she heaved up the contents of her empty stomach.

"I'm going to die," she whimpered as she rested her head on the ground, the sharp pine needles digging into her flesh. It hurt, but she was so weak she couldn't lift her head.

Her basic knowledge of first aid told her she was quickly going into shock. It wouldn't be long before she passed out. Without help soon, she would die. She'd saved Margaret only to die in the process. The irony brought a brief moment of sardonic laughter only to turn into a soft cry of agony.

Slipping deeper, she felt the veil of unconsciousness drawn across her mind, and with one last strain of thought, she prayed to God for help. Then darkness took over.

DETECTIVE BRADLEY CAME OUT OF the sheriff's office and looked at the girls, his expression showing discouragement.

"Oh no," Jess said. "Something is wrong."

"It's going to be okay," Cassie assured her.

Jess appreciated that she was trying to be positive, but the worry inside of her caused tears to form. They couldn't come this far only to fail.

She quickly wiped away her tears and rolled down the window as he walked toward them.

"The sheriff can't be reached at the moment, so we talked to the deputy who has only been there a few months and isn't familiar with all the cabins and their owners. He's trying to reach the sheriff on his two-way but hasn't had any luck."

"What do we do now?"

"Nothing we can do till we talk to the sheriff. There's also another problem. Without a search warrant we can't do anything but locate the cabin and inquire if your friend is there. There are no eyewitnesses that she is in there."

"Can we cross that bridge when we get there?" Cassie asked. "I mean, we have to try and find her. You even admitted that there is something suspicious going on."

"Without snowmobiles we won't make it up any of these roads. They've gotten close to a foot of snow, and even four-wheel drives will have trouble making it."

"While we're waiting for the sheriff, we should be asking around to see if we can borrow some—"

"Landon's calling!" Jess exclaimed when she felt the phone vibrate. "Landon," she answered, "where are you?"

"I have a signal for Emma's phone," he exclaimed. "I've tried calling, but she won't answer."

"What do you mean you have a signal?"

"I have a Find My Phone app, and I programmed her phone into it. I can track her location if her phone has service!"

"Landon, that's amazing!"

"Are you still at the sheriff's office? We're almost there."

"Yes, we're waiting for the sheriff, and they're trying to find snow-mobiles. We won't be able to make it to any of the cabins any other way."

"You're not going to believe this."

"What?"

"My friend who picked me up from the airport has two, and he brought them with him. He figured they might come in handy if we were going to the mountain."

"You're kidding!" Jess couldn't believe what she was hearing.

"What?" Cassie asked, clapping her hands together.

"Hold on," Jess said into the phone then turned to Cassie. "Landon has snowmobiles. He also has an app on his phone that is tracking Emma's phone, and it's receiving a signal that shows Emma's location!"

Cassie let out a whoop of excitement, and Jess asked Landon if there was anything they could do until he arrived.

"Just pray, Jess. Pray that it's not too late!"

Suddenly a commotion from the officers broke out. "Fire!" one of them shouted, pointing off in the distance.

Everyone stopped what they were doing and turned to see dark smoke billowing into the sky.

"Jess, what's going on?" Landon screamed over the phone. "Jess?"

"You'd better hurry," Jess said softly, her heart sinking. "There's a huge fire somewhere, and something tells me it isn't a coincidence."

* * *

Two more snowmobiles were located, and the pack of rescuers pulled on protective gear and teamed up. Extra clothing was located for the girls, and even though it was oversized and smelled like sweat and gasoline the girls didn't care.

Landon took Jess on the back with him, and his friend, Travis, took Cassie on the back with him. The deputy, two assisting officers, and Detective Bradley took the other two machines, and they began the climb up the steep, unplowed road that wound its way deep into the mountain toward the fire.

Jess hung on tight, knowing that if she didn't, one bump would send her flying.

She couldn't forget the look on Landon's face when he finally arrived at the scene where help was gathering to find Emma. She doubted he'd eaten or slept over the last few days and imagined he was existing on pure adrenalin.

Squeezing her eyes shut, she prayed for Emma to be protected and kept safe until they got there. No one knew what the smoke meant, but the fact that it was coming from the direction the cabin was supposedly located gave them all a feeling of alarm.

When she opened her eyes, she noticed that Landon was at the head of the pack and pulling ahead. She couldn't imagine what he was feeling inside, but the way he was driving, she guessed he wasn't about to let anything get in his way of getting to Emma.

Occasionally he pulled out his phone to check the location of Emma's phone.

The road emerged from the tree line and opened to a breathtaking vista across the snow-blanketed valley. It was beautiful, and the pristine snow and startling blue sky created a visual masterpiece. But Jess couldn't stop the growing fear inside as she kept her eye on the sheer drop on the left side of the road as they rounded the bend. She had no idea how far down it went, but sliding off the side of the road was the last thing they needed right now.

The smell of smoke began to seep into her helmet, and she knew they were getting close, the odor making her anxiety escalate.

Trying to navigate the steep grade of the road and the powdery, deep snow made progress difficult, and several times Jess was afraid they weren't going to make it much farther. Somehow Landon managed to coax a little more out of the engine, and the snowmobile roared ahead.

Leading back into the trees, the road finally leveled out, and the group of rescuers plowed ahead, leaving deep troughs in the fresh snow.

As they approached another turn, Jess noticed a large pile of snow up ahead that she soon realized was an automobile covered in snow. She tapped Landon on the shoulder and pointed at the vehicle.

Landon nodded in acknowledgement but didn't slow down. The vehicle wasn't going anywhere; they could investigate later. Getting to Emma was the top priority.

Seconds later they turned the corner and saw the scene of destruction ahead. For the first time, Landon slowed down. The cabin was still ablaze, the roof and top floor a charred skeleton of the former structure.

After taking in the shock of the scene, Landon brought the engine back to life, and they shot forward to get as close to the flaming cabin as possible.

He barely had the machine stopped when he leapt off and started running toward the cabin.

"Landon!" Jess screamed, afraid he was going to go inside.

He came to a stop twenty feet from the blaze then took a few steps back, removing his helmet.

The others arrived, and overhead the sound of a helicopter filled the air.

Jess began crying and praying that Emma was safe.

"Where is she?" Cassie exclaimed, grabbing Jess.

"I don't know, Cassie. I am so scared she didn't get out—"

Jess froze. There was something under the pine tree on the other side of the property.

"Cassie, what's that?" She pointed and started toward the tree then broke into a run. "Landon! I think I found her!" she screamed as she stumbled in the snow.

Cassie helped steady her, and the two friends plowed ahead, the two shapes ahead of them unmoving amidst the noise and confusion.

"Emma!" Landon shouted as he charged ahead of them, his long stride covering the ground faster. He reached the tree first and dove underneath the low-lying branches.

"Emma!" he cried. "Honey, I'm here. Emma!"

Cassie and Jess looked on as Landon scooped Emma into his arms and attempted to get a response from her lifeless form.

He laid her back on the ground and put his face close to hers. Then he put his fingers on her neck to find a pulse.

By then the officers had caught up with him and attended to Margaret who was also lying motionless on the ground. Landon's friend, Travis, knelt down beside him to help.

Jess had to look closely to make sure it really was Emma. It was hard to tell for sure because her hair had been shorn off and she looked gaunt and pale. Judging from Landon's urgent pleadings and efforts to revive her, there was no doubt it was.

"What in the world happened to her?" Cassie said. "That is Emma, isn't it?"

"I think so," Jess responded. "She looks terrible."

"And that's Margaret?"

"Yeah. She doesn't look so great either."

"What in the world happened here?" Cassie asked.

Landon continued to cry out Emma's name, but she still didn't respond. Travis also felt for a pulse and put his cheek close to Emma's mouth and nose, most likely trying to find out if she was breathing.

Tears formed and then spilled onto Jess's cheeks.

One of the officers took out his two-way and called for the helicopter. Even though Emma was wearing a coat, Landon took off his coat and put it over her. One of the officers covered Margaret with his coat. There was no telling how long the two women had been outside.

Jess and Cassie circled arms around each other and watched as Landon, with tears streaming down his face, scooped Emma up in his arms and moved her out from under the tree. Then, with Travis's help, he got to his feet. Travis offered to help carry her, but Landon shook his head and held her tightly in his arms.

Overhead, the helicopter moved into position away from the smoke from the house, and soon a cable holding a rescue basket was lowered.

With the help of the officers, who held the basket steady, Landon placed Emma into the basket then fastened the straps to keep her safe. At Detective Bradley's command, the basket was raised, and the members of the rescue team in the helicopter got Emma safely inside.

As soon as Emma was in the helicopter, Landon was ready to head back down the mountain. He turned to Jess, and by the look on his face, she knew if she wanted a ride she needed to go now.

"I have to be with her. I have to go," he told his friend.

"I'm ready when you are," Travis said.

Landon slid his arms back inside his coat and tried to zip it, but his eyes were so full of tears he couldn't see what he was doing.

"Here," Cassie said, "let me do that."

While Cassie zipped his coat, Jess put an arm around him and tried to assure him everything was going to be okay. She fought back her own tears, trying to stay strong for Landon.

"Her pulse . . . so weak . . . so cold . . ." he sniffed.

"They'll get her warm and take good care of her," Jess assured him.

"I need to go," he said.

"I'm ready," Jess said.

"Travis?"

"I'm ready, buddy. I'll just let the officers know we're leaving."

Leaving the unanswered questions and burning rubble behind, the foursome climbed onto the snowmobiles and turned around to head down the hill.

"Landon," Jess tried to scream over the roar of the engine, "the car." She pointed at the vehicle buried in the snow.

He nodded and stopped the snowmobile. The sun, and possibly heat from the fire, had melted some of the snow and clumps had slid off the sides, exposing the make and model.

"It's yours," she exclaimed.

Travis and Cassie pulled up beside them.

"You want to try and get it out? I think we could pull it with one of these snowmobiles," Travis offered.

"I probably need to, but I don't want to take the time right now."

"If Cassie doesn't mind, we can stay back and try and get it out. You can drive my Jeep home, and we'll bring your car down."

"Sounds good to me," Cassie said. "Whatever I can do to help."

"I can go with you to the hospital," Jess said.

Landon nodded his thanks. "Thanks, Travis."

"Sure thing. We'll call when we get down."

"I'll call you," Jess said to Cassie.

"Give her," Cassie's words caught in her throat, "a hug from me."

"I will," Jess said.

Not wasting another minute, Landon fired up the engine, and the snowmobile shot forward.

* * *

A steady beeping, distant and muffled, broke into Emma's consciousness. She tried to open her eyes, but her lids wouldn't move. When she attempted to lift her hand, she discovered it was strapped down.

"No," she whispered. "Margaret, no." The woman had her tied down to her bed. Who knew what she was going to do to her, or had already done?

Emma quickly became aware of the throbbing in her feet. Had the woman done something to make her wounds even more painful?

"Emma," a voice said, a warm hand covered her own.

As she jerked her hand away, the strap dug into her flesh.

"Shh, it's okay. Honey, it's me, Landon."

An immediate onslaught of emotion overpowered her.

Was she dreaming? Had she actually heard Landon's voice?

"Emma, I'm here."

"Landon," she whispered, quiet sobs shaking her entire body. "Is it really you?"

"Yes, sweetheart, yes. I'm here, and you're safe. Everything is okay."

Tears leaked from the corners of her eyes. She wanted to wipe them away, but her hands were still strapped down.

"Here," Landon said, fumbling with the straps. He set one hand free then the other. "They had to strap you down because you kept trying to fight off something horrible. We were afraid you were going to hurt yourself."

Emma covered her face with her hands and dissolved into body-wracking sobs. Keeping one hand on her face, she reached out the other for Landon.

He took her hand and kissed her palm.

"I thought I died," she said as the wave of emotion subsided.

"Oh, sweetie," he said as he stroked her forehead.

"I can't believe you're here," she said. "The day you left I heard there was a bad storm around Denver. I was so worried something was going to happen to you."

"It was definitely a bumpy flight. I tried to let you know we made it safely."

"How long have I been out?"

"Almost twenty-four hours."

"I don't even remember . . ." Suddenly images of the fire, of Margaret, and of the horrors she suffered in the cabin collided in her mind. She began to cry.

"Shh, honey, it's okay."

Dreams of Margaret attacking her and Emma having to fight her off still lingered in her afterthoughts.

Pulling in several deep breaths, Emma felt some strength return. Finally, she managed to open her eyes. Another flood of tears exploded when she saw Landon's face only inches away from hers.

"I was going crazy," he said, tears welling up in his own eyes. "I didn't know where you were or what had happened to you. I feared the worst, and when we found you, I knew my fears were real. I still don't know what happened to you and Margaret. When we found both of you, I thought you were both dead."

"Is she . . ."

"Fine, she's going to be just fine."

"Good. " She sighed, relieved that Margaret had survived. Did she want that woman behind bars or locked in a facility somewhere? Darn right she did, but she didn't want someone else's blood on her hands.

"You look like you've lost about twenty pounds, and your feet, how in the world did they get cut so badly? And your hair . . . what happened to your hair?"

"You'll never believe what I've been through or what Margaret tried to do to me."

"We have a psychological report of Margaret taken while she was at Whispering Pines. She has some very serious mental issues. Honey, what did Margaret try to do to you?"

"You won't believe me, but it's true." She grabbed at him, feeling her heart rate speed up. The horror was still present in her mind.

"Okay, okay. Slow down. You have time, don't get yourself worked up."

He was right, she was safe, and he was here. He would protect her. She needed to calm down and save her strength. She was so weak and tired.

"Here, how about some water?"

He helped her take some sips of cold water through a straw.

"So good," she said. "More."

The cold, fresh water bathed her parched throat.

"Thank you." She closed her eyes and rested back on her pillow, keeping a tight grip on Landon's hand. "I can't believe you came. I can't believe you're here. I never thought . . ." Emotion overtook her, and she began to sob again.

"Shh, it's okay. Everything is okay."

"I never thought I'd see you again," she whispered.

"I'm here with you now. You're safe. I won't let anything happen to you. Just rest and get your strength back."

"I need to tell you what happened."

He nodded.

"She's crazy. That woman. She's crazy."

"Margaret?"

"Yes. You have to believe me."

"I do, sweetie. I do."

She didn't know where to begin. Just thinking about the cabin and what she'd been through seemed like something out of a bad horror movie.

"I'm sorry to mess up your trip. You're missing everything."

"I wouldn't want to be anywhere else. Being here with you is all that matters."

Landon sat next to her on the bed and pulled her close. She rested her head on his shoulder.

It was over. The horror was over. She was safe now. She was with Landon. A sob ripped from her throat and the dam broke. A flood of tears gushed out of her. And as her emotions settled, she began telling Landon about Margaret tricking her into taking her to the cabin and all the unspeakable, terrifying things she'd done to her.

The purging of emotions left her weak and drained.

"Oh Emma, sweetheart." Landon held her tightly, stroking her hair. "The woman is crazy. There is no way a sane person could do anything like that."

"But there's something I haven't told you. Something worse, something you have to know." She began to cry. "Oh, Landon." She couldn't stop the fresh tears.

"Honey, shh. Everything's going to be okay."

She shook her head. "No. It's bad."

He smoothed the hair back from her forehead and kissed it. "Honey, whatever it is we'll get through together."

"You know how I told you she found out that Jonathan had been with another woman the night he died?"

Landon nodded.

"The woman got pregnant. Margaret found out who she was and paid her a lot of money to agree to give up the baby for adoption after it's born. She wanted me to adopt it."

"What? That's crazy!"

"Yes. She forced me to sign adoption papers, which gratefully got burned in the fire."

"I don't understand how she could—"

"Force me?"

"Well, yeah, I'm sorry, but last time I saw her, she was frail and in a wheelchair."

"I thought the same thing, but it was all an act. Plus she kept me drugged most of the time, and I was weak from lack of water and food."

"Sweetie, I'm not doubting you," he said. "When I first saw you, I thought for sure it was too late, you looked so beat up."

"She's had enough time to plan and prepare for this, so she knew exactly what she needed to do. But there's something else. She knew I wouldn't go along with her adoption plan so she"—a sob caught in her throat—"she . . ."

"Emma?" Landon looked at her with his eyes also filled with tears.

"She gave me injections."

"Injections?"

"Yes, shots of medicine she said forced my body into menopause."

"But why?"

"So I couldn't have children." She burst into tears.

His mouth dropped open. "Is that even possible?"

"If anyone knows drugs and medicine, it's Margaret. She said that maybe if I couldn't have children of my own, then I would agree to raise this child."

"Oh, Emma." He leaned over the bed and circled his arms around her, held her, and assured her everything was going to be okay.

Even though she knew he had no way of knowing any more than she did, it felt comforting to know that they were together and would face the challenge together.

"I think we need to talk to a doctor about this, just so you won't have to worry anymore."

"I would like that."

Landon pushed the Call Nurse button, and a moment later a voice came over the loudspeaker.

"Can I help you?"

"Emma needs to talk to Dr. Madsen as soon as possible."

A knock sounded at the door, and the door cracked open. The doctor looked inside. "Just wanted to check and see how our patient was doing."

"Never mind," Landon told the nurse. "The doctor is here."

"Is everything okay?" Dr. Madsen approached the bed. He held Emma's chart in his hand.

Landon took Emma's hand in his. "Emma just told me that among all the medications Margaret administered to her, she gave her some sort of injection that's supposed to force a woman's body into menopause. Have you ever heard of that?"

The doctor's forehead wrinkled. "Did she say what she gave you?"

Emma nodded. "I've been trying to remember, but I wasn't very clearheaded most of the time. All I know is that the spots where she gave me the shots became swollen and red, really painful."

"Okay," he said thoughtfully, jotting a note on the chart. "Any symptoms?"

"Yes. I had hot flashes and nausea, right off the bat. And I was achy. I had stomach cramps too. At first I thought I had the flu, then she told me what she was doing and why, and I knew she was crazy enough to do something like that."

The doctor's expression showed his concern.

"I was married to her son, her only child, and he died, but before his death, he fathered a child with a woman he was seeing. Margaret wanted me to adopt the child. To add more pressure, she decided to prevent me from having children of my own by giving me these injections, thinking that would make me do what she wanted."

The doctor didn't respond for a moment. Then after clearing his throat, he said, "I'll look into it. There are a couple of medications that come to mind, but I want to do some checking. We'll need to run tests to see if we can determine how much damage the medication did. "

"This has been really upsetting for Emma," Landon said.

"Understandably. I'll see what I can find out."

Just feeling Landon's arms around her, knowing he was there with her, helped the tightness in her muscles dissipate and the tenseness in her stomach calm.

It was over, Emma kept telling herself. She felt herself drifting to sleep, safe in Landon's embrace. But with sleep came darkness and with darkness came the images of Margaret, wielding a syringe, tying her to the bed, chopping off her hair.

"Landon!" she screamed, jerking awake.

"Shh, honey, I'm here. You're safe and everything is okay."

"It was so horrible." She clung to him. "I missed you and prayed you would find me. I prayed constantly. It was the only way I survived."

She began to cry again, but Landon soothed her tears, assuring her he wouldn't leave her.

"She did all those terrible things to me and had more planned, yet when I saw the cabin burning, I knew she would die if I didn't save her. I had to save her."

"I know, sweetie. You risked your life to save her; you could have both died. She owes you her life."

It was so ironic. Margaret had injured her and mistreated her, was even willing to kill her if she needed to, yet Emma couldn't bear letting the woman burn to death.

"I'm sorry about your car."

"Don't you worry about that. The car is fine. Travis and Cassie were able to drive it back."

"Good," she said, closing her eyes and resting again, but her mind began to race with questions. She pushed herself away so she could look at him. "How did you find us?"

"Well, I knew something was wrong that first day, when you didn't answer your phone. I hoped that you'd just forgotten to turn it on or that the battery was dead, but the next morning when I tried again and you didn't answer, I began to panic. I started making calls. Then I heard from Jess. She and Cassie had also been trying to reach you."

"I tried to leave messages before I lost cell service."

"Nobody got the message until you left the mountain, then they went through. Funny, though, there was a 911 call from your phone reported, but the report said there was no response."

"The second day we were there, the day I drove your car off the road, I had service, for just a minute. I called but lost service before I could say anything,"

"That must have been awful."

"It was so close. If I could have made a connection, I could have had them send help."

"Well, you should be very grateful you have two very persistent friends. They never gave up looking. I think they should go into private investigating together. They made a good team."

"I'm confused. Jess told me she didn't like Cassie, something about Cassie stealing her boyfriend in high school."

"You wouldn't know it now. They are inseparable."

"I need to see them. I need to thank them. Who knows what would be going on right now if they hadn't been so persistent."

"After you didn't show up for lunch, Jess got worried. She said she'd gone by your house and you weren't there and that she looked in the windows and couldn't see anything out of the ordinary. She got a hold of Cassie, and together they decided that something was definitely wrong."

"I'm so glad they figured it out."

"Me too. When they called I was about out of my mind with worry. They kept in contact with me while they were digging around. I was about to call the police when the thought occurred to me that maybe Margaret knew where you were. I knew she kept close tabs on you daily, so I figured she might know something. That's when I got really worried. The director of the care center told me you had come to check her out."

"Which I never did. I didn't sign any sort of release."

"According to them her attorney had taken care of everything, naming you primary caregiver."

"I never would agree to that."

"Cassie and Jess tried to find her attorney, but he's disappeared. I don't know how Margaret pulled all of this off."

"It helps to be conniving and manipulative. She's been planning this for months. She caught me off guard because I didn't know she was leaving the facility for good. I knew something was wrong when she made me go out the side entrance, but I didn't want to upset her by asking questions."

"You'll have a chance to tell the police everything. Don't get yourself worked up." He placed his hands on her arms to help her settle down. "It's all going to be fine, sweetie. You need to stay calm."

She collapsed back and squeezed her eyes shut, causing tears to fall.

Landon stroked her forehead and smoothed back her hair. "Honey, I'm here now. Everything's going to be okay."

She nodded. "I know. I'm sorry." She pulled in several shaky breaths. "I suppose I know why my arms were strapped down.

"You must have been having some pretty horrible dreams the way you were thrashing around."

"I was reliving it, the head games and manipulation, all the pain and fear she caused me. I'm going to need therapy for the rest of my life!" Her hands balled up into fists. "And the worst part is I didn't do anything to deserve it!"

"I know, honey—"

"You know what, I need to talk to her. Where is that woman," Emma said, pushing herself up off the bed. "I need some answers from her!"

Landon stroked her shoulder. "She's in another room. She hasn't woken up yet."

"I'll wake her up!"

"You'll have a chance to talk to her, I promise."

"It probably won't do any good, anyway." She spit the words. "She is so demented and crazy she probably still thinks she didn't do anything wrong. And she manages to make everyone else believe her!"

"Not everyone. Cassie and Jess told me that one of the employees who helped them gave them a copy of a report. The doctors at Whispering Pines had just done some tests on her and diagnosed her as, let me see if I can get this right, obsessive-compulsive with greater emphasis on the narcissistic personality disorder."

"What! They knew she was a nut-job and they let her leave?"

"The employee said that was why she left. When the test came back, she didn't waste any time making arrangements to get out of there. She met with her attorney and got the release papers drawn up."

"She's gone over the edge. I know she's not well and I know she's been through a lot with her husband's death and Jonathan's death, but to think of what she put me through and that she actually expected me to adopt Jonathan's illegitimate baby . . ."

It took a few minutes for Landon to calm her down, but Emma finally managed to relax. Her little tirade wore her out.

Within minutes her eyelids grew heavy. Her body demanded rest.

"Honey," Landon said softly, "I need to make some work calls and notify the officer working on the case that you're ready to make a statement. I'm going to step outside so you can sleep. You going to be okay?"

She nodded. "You'll be outside?"

"You want me to bring back anything?"

"Yes, I'm starving. I would love a turkey sandwich and a berry smoothie if they have one. And potato chips."

"Barbecue?"

"Of course."

Landon chuckled and gave her a hug. "I'll hurry. Just relax and get your strength back."

Emma couldn't relax. She kept thinking about her ordeal. "I'm so mad at myself for not seeing what she was capable of. I should have figured it out."

Landon shook his head. "She had me fooled too. Your story is going to come as a surprise to a lot of people."

"I just hope they believe me."

"They will. Don't worry."

Landon gave her a kiss before he got up to leave. "I'm so glad you're okay."

"Prayer and wanting to be with you again kept me going. There were a few times I wasn't sure I was going to survive."

He cleared his throat. "I don't know what I would have done if something would have happened to you."

She bit her lip to help her keep her emotions and nodded, still trying to believe her ordeal was over and she was with Landon.

"You okay?" he asked, taking a step toward her.

She nodded. "Yes. Hurry though. I don't want to be alone very long."

"I will."

He turned to leave but didn't move.

"Is something wrong?"

"I just realized something." He turned back around.

She tried to read his expression but wasn't sure if it was sadness or disappointment. "Landon, you're scaring me."

"I forgot to get chocolate." His shoulders slumped.

She laughed. "Is that all? I can get chocolate anytime."

"Are you sure?"

"Tell you what." She reached for his hand. He walked back and took a hold of it. "Maybe next time I'll go and get it with you."

His eyebrows arched with surprise. "Really? After all this you're ready to hop on a plane now?"

"Well, maybe not right now, but I'm done letting my fears control my life."

He shook his head, a smile grew on his face. "You know, one of the last things you said to me when I left for Europe was something about getting feisty."

"I did, didn't I?"

"I'll tell you what, whenever you're ready, we'll go to Switzerland. I know the perfect little shop in Geneva that sells the best chocolate in the world."

They sealed the deal with a kiss.

A feeling of anxiousness set her heart thumping when he left, but she closed her eyes and forced herself to calm down. She tried to focus on all the good about her future with Landon.

Visions of their temple sealing and a reception with family and friends helped her calm down. In her mind she could see the garden reception they had planned. The beautiful flowers, the three-tiered cake, the dress, and her future husband, dressed in a tuxedo, smiling at her. The thought brought a smile to her lips and joy to her heart. She was going from living a nightmare to having a dream come true. A constant prayer of gratitude ran through her mind. She had been watched over, protected. She knew that without a doubt.

Peace rested upon her, and she allowed herself to drift into a much needed sleep.

Her peaceful rest didn't last long. Soon, thunder and lightning began as she ran to find shelter. Her lungs burned as she ran through the trees, knowing she needed a safe place to wait out the storm. Finally she saw a small building, like a groundskeeper shed, but when she tried to open the door or window, she found them all locked. Luckily there was an overhang and a small space she could step into that would protect her from the violent storm.

Her safe place wasn't safe for long. Soon she felt confined and felt her arms pinned to her sides. Instead of standing, she was lying down, and when she lifted her head, she saw she was in a cemetery. "Help!" she cried. "Please, help!"

A face appeared before her, but it was out of focus. "Please," she asked the person, "will you help me?"

"Of course, my dear." The voice sounded like the witch from *Snow White and the Seven Dwarfs*. The witch's face appeared and distorted as she began to cackle.

Emma turned her head and shut her eyes, but the laugh continued.

"I will help you," the voice said again, but this time it wasn't the witch's voice she heard. It was Margaret's.

She was no longer in the cemetery, but in the hospital bed. And she was no longer asleep.

Terrified to open her eyes, she knew she wasn't alone and that Margaret was in the room with her.

"There now," Margaret said. "Everything is going to be just fine."

The woman touched Emma's arm, causing Emma to jump. Her eyes flew open.

"What are you doing in here?" Emma asked. Where was Landon? He'd stepped out to make phone calls and go get food. Why wasn't he back yet?

"Shh," Margaret said. "Not so loud. This will probably be our last chance to talk."

"Why are my arms strapped down again?"

"You were throwing your arms about. I worried you were going to pull out your IV or injure yourself."

Emma didn't want to show her she was frightened, but she was. This woman had proven she was capable of anything. "You need to leave. Landon will be back any minute."

"Oh, how sweet. Your fiancé is here."

"Margaret, you have to let go. I'm moving on. Jonathan is gone. Accept it."

Margaret dropped her chin and nodded. "You're right. I do. I have acted irrationally and out of desperation, and I'm sorry. I was so terrified of losing the one person I could count on. I was so afraid you would get married and forget about me."

Emma didn't know what to say. The woman had made it impossible for them to continue any sort of relationship.

"Don't think I couldn't tell how painful it was for you to come and visit me every time. I knew you didn't want to be there."

"That's not true. We've never had a good relationship, but I was willing to try."

"That's not how it seemed to me. Even the nurses at the care center mentioned how you seemed to resent having to come and visit me."

Emma opened her mouth to protest but knew it was futile. Margaret believed what she wanted to believe.

"I suppose you're going to tell the police how you knew my health was bad and assumed I was going to leave everything to you when I died. But when you found out I was leaving it to my sister, you decided to take me somewhere to convince me to change my will."

"Huh? I don't know what you're talking about. That's not true, and you know it."

"Maybe so, but who are the police going to believe? A little old lady who uses a walker and lives in a care center, or you, a gold digger who nagged your husband for material things until he couldn't take it anymore?"

"That's not true!"

"As far as the police are concerned, it is. I can't have you telling them things that will make me look bad and bring shame to my family."

She pulled out a syringe.

"Margaret, what do you think you're going to do?"

"I'm going to stop you before you say anything."

"I saved your life!"

"That was your choice. I wouldn't have been in danger if you hadn't injected me."

"Please, Margaret, please think about what you're doing."

"Oh, I have. I knew exactly what I was going to do if my first plan didn't work out. Do you realize I was going to give you everything, even a child? We could have kept the family name going. You've ruined everything."

She lifted the syringe to the IV. "I didn't want to have to resort to this, but if you won't live the life I planned, I'm afraid I can't let you live at all. All I wanted was for you to raise your husband's child, my grandchild. My flesh and blood!"

"Margaret, don't do this. They'll know it was you," Emma said.

"Doubtful. Unless they know to look for potassium chloride, they won't suspect a thing. You've been through a traumatic experience. You're recovering from severe shock and exposure; it's not uncommon for the heart to stop functioning."

Emma knew what she needed to do. "Tell me, Margaret, is it also common to do this?" Margaret looked at her with a confused expression, and Emma began screaming for help at the top of her lungs.

The sudden explosion of noise threw Margaret off for a moment, but she quickly regained her sense of purpose and thrust the syringe into the IV connector, delivering a lethal dose of medication.

Emma continued screaming as Margaret slipped from the room. Her focus changed when she realized she needed to somehow stop the fluid in the IV bag from flowing into her veins. In the following seconds, she tried to grab the tube that fed into her arm with her mouth, twisting her head to get a hold of it. Finally, using her tongue she managed to snag the tube then bit down hard on it, clamping it shut.

A nurse burst into the room. "What's going on in here?"

Emma screamed help through her clenched teeth.

The nurse rushed to her side. "What are you doing?" She tried to pry the tube from Emma's mouth.

Trying to tell her no but not getting the nurse to understand, Emma pulled her knees up to her chest then gave the nurse a shove with her feet, causing the nurse to stumble backwards and crash into a chair and tumble to the floor. The impact on Emma's injured feet caused her to cry out in pain, but her teeth held fast to the tube.

Within another second, Landon charged into the room followed by a police officer and a doctor.

"Emma, what's going on?"

The doctor tried to work the tube from her mouth. "She must be having some kind of reaction. Hold her down so I can get that IV tube out of her mouth."

"No!" Emma tried to scream through her clenched teeth.

Landon pushed her shoulders onto the bed, and the policeman held down her feet.

The doctor pulled on the tube as hard as he could and managed to free it from her teeth, but water was dripping from the section Emma had in her mouth.

"Margaret was in here!" Emma screamed. "She put some sort of medicine in the IV."

"What?" Landon asked in disbelief.

"Get it out of my arm!" she yelled, trying to grab the tube with her mouth again.

"Wait," the doctor said to Landon. "She's having a reaction. We need to administer a sedative to calm her down."

"Landon, I'm not having a reaction. If you don't take it out, I will die."

Landon looked at her, then at the doctor, then back at her.

Before the doctor could stop him, Landon reached down and ripped the tape off her arm and yanked out the needle in her vein.

"Why did you do that?" the doctor demanded. "Nurse!" he yelled.

"Thank you!" Emma said, and she began to sob.

"Emma, what's going on?" Landon asked. He leaned over her, spreading an arm across her, as if to protect her.

"Margaret came in. She injected something into my IV. She said it was potassium, um, chro—, clo—, uh. I don't remember. She said it would stop my heart!"

"Potassium chloride?" the doctor asked.

"Yes! Yes, that's it." Emma relaxed. "Yes!"

"Is it true?" Landon asked. "Could it stop her heart?"

"Without a doubt," the doctor said. "It's one of the lethal injection drugs used to execute prisoners. It's a good thing you listened to her," he told Landon.

"Someone needs to find her!" Emma cried.

"I'll notify the department," Officer Colton said and rushed from the room.

"Nurse, call security," the doctor ordered. "We need to find out how that woman got a hold of that syringe and medication."

"Right away, doctor."

"Emma, how are you feeling?" He felt her wrist for a pulse and then listened to her heart with his stethoscope.

"I'm fine, I think. I'm probably going to have issues for the rest of my life. This woman has tormented and terrorized me too many times."

"I won't let you be alone," Landon said. "I promise."

"Your quick thinking saved your life," the doctor said. "You're a good little fighter."

"I kicked the nurse. I need to tell her I'm sorry."

"She'll be back so you can tell her. I'm sure she'll understand."

"I almost kicked you," Emma said.

"I would have deserved it. "

"I'm so glad you believed me," Emma said to Landon.

The doctor nodded. "It's a good thing you did."

Landon took Emma's hand and held on tightly.

"Margaret needs to be locked up," Landon said. "She is extremely dangerous."

The door opened and the policeman who had been there a few minutes earlier stepped back into the room. "We're posting an officer outside the door."

"Why?" Landon asked.

"Margaret Lowell left the hospital."

13

"CASSIE, I FEEL TERRIBLE THAT you have to come and babysit me while Landon is at work." Emma stirred her cup of hot cocoa and sprinkled some mini marshmallows on top. Getting food and rest had done wonders for her. She also had a security guard outside her front door, which helped her feel safe.

"Are you kidding? I was thrilled to have a chance to spend some time with you and catch up. I thought maybe to help distract you we could look at houses online and come up with a list of homes to look at when you're ready. I can also stay overnight if you need me to."

"That's really sweet of you. Jess said she can take some time off work and stay all week if I need her too. I feel like such a baby, but I'm just not ready to be alone yet." She broke off a small piece of the raspberry Danish Cassie had brought her and ate it.

"Hey, I totally understand. You've been through some serious stuff. I don't think anyone blames you for being nervous to be alone." She took a sip of her cocoa. "Still no sign of Margaret?"

"No, she completely disappeared. It's been almost forty-eight hours since she went missing."

"She could be anywhere. Do they know if she's here in the Seattle area?"

"As far as I know, they don't."

"You're probably not going to be able to rest until they have Margaret in custody."

Emma shook her head and shivered. "I can't. I picture her popping out of the shadows and from behind doors. I'm telling you, Cassie, you wouldn't believe what this old woman is capable of. I keep trying to figure out where she would go. She was on foot; she didn't have any money with her; she didn't have warm clothes."

"Could she be getting help from someone?"

Emma didn't say anything. Before she left Emma at the hospital, the last thing Margaret talked about was her grandchild.

Cassie waited for a response for a few moments then waved her hand in front of Emma's face. "Hello. You okay?"

"Cassie, this could be bad."

"What? Emma, what do you think is going on?"

"We have to warn that girl."

"What girl?"

"The one carrying Jonathan's baby."

"Carrying what? What baby?"

"I can't explain now. But I think I know where Margaret is," Emma said, trying to reach her phone.

"You do? Where? Here, let me help you."

"Hand me my phone! I need to call the police. I hope we're not too late!"

Cassie handed Emma's phone to her. "Too late for what?"

Emma didn't have a chance to answer the question.

"Officer Colton," the policeman said.

"This is Emma Lowell. I think I know where Margaret went." Cassie's face registered shock while Emma explained everything to Officer Colton. When Emma finished, the officer told her to stand by and he'd call her back as soon as they located a last-known address for the woman.

Emma hung up and quickly dialed Landon. She really needed him there. His phone went to voice mail. She left a message for him to call.

"How did you find out about the baby?" Cassie asked.

"Oh, well, Margaret was planning on buying the baby and having me adopt it to raise as my own. She wasn't about to let one of the Lowell offspring out of her reach."

"What? She wasn't serious!"

Emma pointed to her heavily bandaged feet.

"I don't believe it! And you think she's gone over to the house to do what?"

"I don't know, kidnap her or something? The baby isn't due for a few more weeks, so she can't take the child. I don't know, but that's definitely where she's headed!"

Her phone vibrated. It was Landon.

"I'm on my way. What's going on?"

She told him, and he agreed the pregnant woman was probably Margaret's next target. He told her he was only a few minutes away, and they hung up.

"I wonder what's taking Officer Colton so long," Cassie said. "You don't think Margaret would hurt her, do you? I mean, she is pregnant."

"I don't think she'd do anything to hurt the child," Emma said. "So the mother should be safe, right?"

Her phone buzzed with an incoming text. It was Jess.

"Will you call Jess and tell her what's going on? I don't want to tie up my phone."

Cassie made the call, and Emma watched her phone for Officer Colton's call. The woman's name had to be in the police report that was taken after Jonathan's death. She prayed they weren't too late. Margaret's state of mind was questionable, and Emma knew all too well what she was capable of.

"Jess is on her way over too. She can't focus at work with all that's going on."

Emma nodded and looked at her phone again, like that would make it ring any faster. "I hate sitting here! But I wouldn't even know where to go."

Cassie looked out the window. "Landon's here."

"Oh good." Emma always felt better when he was with her.

He was at the door in seconds. "Have you heard anything?"

"Not yet," Emma said.

Landon came over and gave her a kiss. "How are you doing?"

"I'm kicking myself for not thinking of this sooner. I should have known Margaret would go after this woman. I should have figured this out before now."

"You've barely had time to process any of this," he said. "Let's just hope nothing bad has happened. Maybe Margaret's just looking for a place to hide."

"I hope you're—" Her phone vibrated with an incoming call. "It's Officer Colton." She answered the call.

"Miss Lowell, this is Officer Colton. Your hunch was right. We believe Margaret Lowell did go to the residence of a Miss Desiree Francis."

"What do you mean, you believe?"

"We had an officer in the area where Miss Francis lives, so he was able to check immediately. The officer found Miss Francis unconscious. There was a syringe next to her. We're afraid she was injected with the same medication Mrs. Lowell gave you in the hospital."

"Is she going to live? Is the baby okay?"

"We don't know yet. She has been transported to the hospital. If we'd been much later though, there's no question both she and the baby would have been dead."

Emma could barely speak. She had to take a breath and clear the emotion from her throat. "Will you please let me know as soon as you hear anything?"

"Of course. In the meantime, is there anywhere else you can think of that Margaret would go?"

"No, but if I do, I'll let you know." Emma ended the call and sent up a prayer for Desiree and her baby. If only she'd thought of them sooner. How could Margaret do that? Why would she risk the unborn child's life like that? Unless . . .

"Emma?" Landon's voice broke through her thoughts. "Honey, what did he say?"

Emma told them, unable to stop her tears.

"How could she?" Cassie said. "How could any woman injure a pregnant woman?"

"I bet I know what happened," Emma said. "I'll bet Desiree told her she changed her mind and wasn't going to let Margaret have the baby. That would do it. Margaret said she wasn't going to let a woman like that raise her grandchild."

Landon shook his head. "Honey, are you okay?"

He knelt down beside her and gathered her in his arms. She buried her head in his neck and cried. "If anything happens to them . . ."

"Honey, you probably saved their lives."

"I hope you're right."

Cassie handed her a tissue. "So do they have any idea where Margaret is now?"

"No, none. Where could she possibly be?" Emma dried her tears. Her head was beginning to hurt. "She has nowhere to go. She doesn't have a home anymore. She has no family. Everyone she loved is gone. There's nothing left for her but . . ."

Landon and Cassie looked at her, waiting for her to finish.

"Honey?" Landon said.

"This is a long shot, but I have another idea about where Margaret might go."

She tried to get up.

"You're not supposed—" Cassie started to say.

"We have to go!" she said, placing a call to Officer Colton.

"Here." Landon handed her crutches to Cassie. "You take these, I'll take her."

* * *

The entrance to the cemetery was strewn with brown, withered vines and dead leaves. The recent winter storms had brought plenty of rain with a mix of snow and ice.

Emma had visited Jonathan's gravesite once since he'd passed away. After she and Landon had gotten engaged she'd felt some kind of obligation to tell Jonathan. Get closure. It had worked. She had left and never looked back again.

Jonathan and his father were buried next to each other. There were two more plots beside them; one for Margaret and one for Emma. In fact, Margaret's name was already on the headstone with her husband's. She'd wanted to put Emma's name on Jonathan's, but Emma had put her foot down. It was the only time Margaret had listened to her.

The headstones couldn't be seen from the road, so they would have a short distance to walk to get there.

As soon as they stopped the cars, Landon jumped out and came to Emma's side of the car.

"Do you think we should wait for the police?"

She shook her head. "No, we have to go now."

His eyebrows arched in question.

"Please, I don't want to wait."

With Landon's help she got out of the car and got her crutches, and they began the walk to the gravesites.

They didn't speak but walked as quickly as Emma could go on crutches. She felt the muscles in her stomach bunch with anticipation of what they would encounter.

"Almost there," she said. The graves were near the edge of a wooded area, a beautiful, picturesque section of the cemetery.

The path directed them over a small bridge crossing an empty stream, and Emma strained to look for the familiar gray, rectangular headstones.

"Oh no!" Emma whispered, stopping dead in her tracks.

Ahead of them was a woman's body curled up between the two stones.

"Um, I don't think I can go over there," Cassie said, backing away.

"We should wait for the police," Landon said.

On the road behind them, Emma heard the screech of tires.

"They're here! Let's go."

The three moved as quickly as Emma could, the police coming up behind them.

"Is it Margaret?" Cassie asked.

"I want to talk to her before the police take her." Emma was ready to confront the woman. Emma needed to show Margaret that her plan had failed. "But if she starts running, Landon, you have to tackle her."

"What?"

"Trust me, she's freakishly strong!"

"She looks dead," Cassie said.

"The woman has nine lives. She's not dead!" Emma said.

"All right, let's just do this. I'll go ahead," Landon said.

"Be careful. You never know what she will do. We'll be right behind you."

Landon rolled his shoulders back and expanded his chest with a big breath then he began walking.

As they got closer, Cassie whispered, "Aren't you scared?"

Emma didn't miss a step. "No. I'm not going to let her hurt me anymore."

The older woman didn't move when they approached. Cassie and Emma hung back while Landon took several slow, deliberate steps toward her.

"Margaret," he said softly.

She didn't answer.

He said her name louder and got closer.

Emma prepared herself for Margaret to rise up like a monster from a horror movie and swallow him whole, but nothing happened. She didn't move.

"Is she . . . ?" Emma couldn't finish.

"I can't tell. She isn't moving. Her coloring looks bad too."

He knelt beside Margaret and felt for a pulse.

"It's faint, but I think she's still alive."

Cassie slipped an arm around Emma. "You okay?"

Emma nodded.

Voices from the approaching officers echoed through the trees.

Landon came back and stood beside her with an arm around her waist. "You sure you're okay?"

"Yeah, I'm good."

Three officers joined them and called for an ambulance. Within minutes the ambulance arrived and a team of medics worked quickly, addressing the immediate concerns of exposure and dehydration. Emma didn't catch everything that was going on, but the intensity and speed with which the men operated showed how dire the situation really was.

As they moved Margaret onto the gurney, she began to stir, mumbling and reaching out.

The EMTs continued their duties, but Margaret seemed agitated and desperate to communicate with them.

Finally, one of the men said, "She keeps asking for someone named Emma."

Emma grabbed Landon's arm.

"I'm Emma," she told him.

"She acts like she wants to tell you something." The guy looked at her with a questioning gaze.

Emma was frozen in position.

"You'd better hurry, lady. She needs to get to a hospital fast."

"Come with me," she said to Landon.

The EMT stepped aside and let Emma get next to her. "Margaret, I'm here."

Margaret's face bunched up, and she shook her head. Then, with a shaky breath, she opened her eyes, which were filled with tears, and looked at Emma. "Emma, you're alive. I can't believe it! I am so sorry . . ." She paused for a moment. "I am so sorry I didn't kill you." She reached her hand toward Emma, but Emma stepped back out of her reach.

Emma looked at the pathetic old woman and said, "Get her out of my sight."

"Let's go," one of the other EMTs said.

"You can meet us at the hospital," the medic who stepped aside told her.

Emma watched, with Landon's arm firmly around her, as they loaded Margaret into the back of the ambulance. The ambulance pulled away, and the police officers went to the gravestones to look around.

"You want to go to the hospital?" Landon asked.

"No, let's go home. My feet hurt."

"Here," Landon said, sweeping her off her feet.

"I'll take those," Cassie said, grabbing the crutches.

"I can walk," Emma insisted.

"Shh," Cassie told her. "It's not every day you get an offer like that."

"I want to check on Desiree and her baby," Emma said. "And Jess—we need to call Jess."

"Landon, you've got your hands full," Cassie said. "I'll take care of the calls."

Emma's heart filled with gratitude for her sweetheart and her dear friends. As messed up as all of this was, she knew she could handle it with their love and support. It would probably take years to sort out what had happened and all the emotions that were going on inside of her. Margaret undoubtedly suffered from serious psychological problems. The woman was disturbed, violent, and dangerous, yet even after what she'd said, Emma felt compassion for her. Perhaps it was because she had known what it was like to not have a family or loved ones to lean on. The thought of not having Landon and dear friends in her life gave her a feeling of panic and anxiety. Emma's pending marriage had thrown Margaret into a complete meltdown, and she was convinced that she was going to lose Emma.

"You okay?" Landon asked.

Emma nodded. "Surprisingly, yes. It's hard to explain. I'm terrified of what Margaret did and said, but she wasn't well and she was desperate."

"Who knows what would've happened, though, if you hadn't finally escaped and we found you when we did," he reminded her.

"I know, but I have to forgive her. I couldn't live with the alternative."

Landon gave her an understanding smile. "You amaze me, honey."

"It isn't me. I have some heavenly help."

By the time they got back to her house, Emma had a whole new appreciation for the remarkable man she was going to marry. He listened to her share her feelings and thoughts, and gave love and support in return.

"I'll call you later," Cassie told her. "Jess wondered if we could bring dinner over."

"I'd love that," Emma said, giving her friend a hug. "Thank you for being there for me."

"Of course. That's what friends are for."

Cassie left, and Landon helped Emma get comfortable on the couch.

He went to get them both a drink of ice water when her phone rang. It was Officer Colton. "Landon! Officer Colton is calling," she told him. Then she answered the call. "Hello?"

"Miss Lowell, I thought I'd better give you an update. You're going to find out soon enough."

"Do you mind if I put you on speakerphone? My fiancé is here with me."

"Not at all. I just wanted to let you know that on the way to the hospital, Margaret Lowell went into cardiac arrest. The paramedics did everything they could."

"She died?" Landon asked.

Emma's breath caught in her throat.

"She did," the officer said.

"Wow." She breathed the word. "She's gone."

Landon slipped an arm around her shoulder. "Have you heard anything about Desiree and the baby?"

The officer didn't answer immediately. Emma knew the news wasn't good.

"I'm really sorry to dump all of this on you at once. Miss Francis is in a coma and is in the ICU. They delivered the baby by Caesarean section. He didn't make it."

Emma's heart dropped. Immediately tears filled her eyes and tumbled onto her cheeks.

"Thank you, Officer. We appreciate you calling."

Landon ended the call, circled Emma in his arms, and let her cry. That poor innocent baby boy. It was almost too much to bear.

All the exhaustion and emotions left her feeling completely drained. She prayed for Desiree, for peace, and for Margaret's soul. She was grateful it was out of her hands and out of her life now.

It was over.

EPILOGUE

"EMMA, WHERE DO YOU WANT this lamp?" Cassie asked, holding up a polished silver lamp base with a cream colored shade. "And these pillows? On the couch?"

Emma glanced over from the bookshelf where she was unloading boxes. "Pillows on the couch, but the lamp goes in the extra bedroom," she told her. She placed a stack of her photography books next to Landon's travel books, pausing to look at the picture of the Eiffel Tower on the front of the Paris book they bought on their honeymoon.

"Hey, aren't you supposed to be resting with your feet up?" Jess said as she stacked some empty boxes together. "Landon said the only way he dared go to San Francisco for the day was if you didn't lift a finger. That's why we're here."

"I feel great, and at the rate I'm going, this baby is never coming out!"

"Still, you don't want to take a chance and have it before Landon gets home"—Jess glanced at her watch—"and that's not for another two hours."

"The contractions I had earlier have stopped. I might as well get some work done. Besides, with your help we've almost finished every room. Landon's not going to believe it." She reached down to grab another handful of books and stopped abruptly, bracing herself against the burgundy wingback chair next to the bookshelf. A groan escaped her lips.

Jess dropped the boxes she was taking out to the recycling bin. "What is it, Emma? What are you doing?"

"I'm . . . fine . . . I think," Emma said, breathing through the excrutiating contraction. She shut her eyes as the tightness in her abdomen and lower back increased. She moaned, trying to be brave, while her knees began to buckle.

"Cassie!" Jess called as she stepped over boxes to get to her friend.

"What's going on?" Cassie rushed into the room.

"She's having a hard contraction," Jess said, wringing her hands. "I don't know what to do."

"Emma, honey, how can we help?" Cassie hurried to Emma's side.

Emma held up her hand to let them know she didn't need help. She was going to be fine. The baby wasn't due for another week.

"Okay, all better." She paused to take some deep breaths as the pain began to subside. "They told me not to come until the contractions were five minutes apart. I gotta admit, though, that's the worst one so far."

Cassie and Jess exchanged worried looks.

"It's okay. I promise."

Cassie glanced at her watch. "I'll start timing them."

"Here," Jess said, taking a box off of the chair, "you need to sit."

"I promise I'm fine."

"You didn't look fine," Jess said. "Will you please sit down like we promised Landon?"

"Just one more box?"

"Sorry. If he asks, I want to be able to tell him you were putting your feet up, not unloading boxes," Jess told her.

Their expressions told Emma there was no convincing them.

"Besides, these boxes aren't going anywhere. If it is a false alarm, you can resume working when he gets home," Cassie told her.

Jess helped lift Emma's feet onto a footstool. "There, isn't that better."

"Yes, but I feel guilty."

"Are you kidding? When I'm pregnant someday, I will expect nothing but pampering," Cassie said.

Emma laughed. "You know, now that you mention it, I would like my toenails painted."

"Where's your polish?" Jess asked.

"I'm kidding. I've got a pedicure appointment in the morning."

"You don't look comfortable," Cassie noticed. "Do you need a pillow behind your back?"

"That would be nice." Emma leaned forward while Cassie slid a small accent pillow behind her. "Thanks, that's better. I felt the pain in my lower back. Is that weird to have back labor?"

"I don't think so," Cassie said. "I remember a couple of my sisters saying that's where they felt their labor with some of their deliveries."

"Can I get you anything?" Jess offered. "Something to drink?"

"NO!" Cassie snapped. "Sorry, but if she's going into labor, she shouldn't have anything."

"Sorry, I didn't know." Jess's expression showed alarm.

"Thanks, Jess," Emma said. "She's right. But you don't have to worry. I'm not going into labor."

"It made my toes curl just watching the pain on your face," Jess said.

"One of my sister's labor went so fast," Cassie told her, "they didn't have time to give her anesthesia. I was in the room with her, and I'm telling you—"

Wanting to change the subject, Emma said, "So Cassie, have you heard from Sean since you broke up with him?"

"Uh, yeah. He's texted me a couple of times, but I haven't responded."

"I feel so bad. He seems like such a great guy," Emma said.

"Don't get me wrong," Cassie responded, "he is a great guy, and I didn't even care that he was dating someone else, we weren't exclusive or anything, but the fact that he lied about it is what bothers me. I mean, there was no reason—"

"Owww!" Emma's lower back muscles seized up, and she leaned forward putting her hands on her knees for support.

"That was barely four minutes!" Cassie cried. "That's it. We are leaving!"

The tightening in her back crawled around to the front of her stomach. It felt like an anaconda was wrapped around her, squeezing the life out of her. Trying to remember her breathing techniques, Emma stared at the picture of the Eiffel Tower and regulated her breathing. Focusing on the picture, she thought about her time with Landon in Paris, the food, the sights, and the pure bliss of walking the streets hand in hand, drinking in the romance of the city.

She blocked Jess and Cassie's frenzied jabbering from her mind and kept her focus and breathing as the contraction subsided. When it finished she looked at both of her friends' faces. "What?" she said.

"You did great. That was amazing," Cassie said.

"It really was. Where were you just then?" Jess asked.

Emma laughed. "Paris."

"Ah!" Jess closed her eyes. "It sounds so wonderful. That's where I want to go for my—"

"What are we doing standing here?" Cassie exclaimed. "Four minutes is one less than five, people!"

"But, I want to wait till Landon—"

"He's going to have to meet us there. These contractions mean business."

Jess agreed. "I've never been around someone in labor, but these seem really different from those Braxton Hicks thingies you've been having."

Emma took a deep breath and blew it out. "Okay. But if they send me home . . ." She didn't want to freak out her friends, but that last contraction hurt so badly it scared her for what was ahead. She prayed Landon would hurry; she didn't want baby Oliver to be born before his daddy got there.

"We need to call Landon," she said.

"I'll call him right now. Jess, can you open the door?"

Jess scooped up the overnight bag and Emma's purse, which was right next to it, then swung the door wide open while Cassie helped Emma outside.

"Careful on the stairs," Cassie said.

Jess pulled the door shut then came up beside her and gave assistance. "This is so exciting, Em. It's finally happening."

Emma gave her a smile, appreciating both of her friends' help and enthusiam. They were there for her whenever she needed them. She would always be in their debt. Had they not searched for answers and helped the authorities locate her, Emma doubted she would have survived Margaret's cabin.

The story had been covered by the local news programs and newspapers and then caught the attention of several national papers. A national morning show had approached her about coming on and talking about her ordeal, but Emma was ready to move on and have the attention fade away. It was time to start her life fresh and new with Landon.

At her wedding, Cassie and Jess were Emma's co–maids of honor. She could have never chosen between them. They were both key in helping save her from a horrible fate; she wanted them there beside her on the happiest day of her life.

"We'll be there before you know it!" Cassie said as she drove the car toward the freeway on-ramp. "We shouldn't have too much traffic this time of night."

Emma glanced at the clock. It was almost seven. Landon wasn't scheduled to arrive until eight thirty or nine.

He hadn't wanted to go on the trip, but she'd practically made him. She had been convinced nothing would happen. She prayed it wouldn't.

The car roared onto the freeway with Cassie pushing the speed limit as she negotiated from lane to lane.

"Uh-oh, here we go again," Emma said through gritted teeth.

"It's going to be okay," Cassie assured her increasing the speed of the car. "Just breathe and focus."

"Hee-hee-hee-ho," Emma said through ragged breaths, gripping the armrest in the car. The pain escalated, causing her to cry out as tears leaked out of her eyes. "Is Landon going to make it?"

"I left a message on his voice mail. I'm sure he'll make it," Jess said. "Cassie, hurry!"

"I am. I don't want to have an accident! We're almost there, Em. Hang in there."

Emma nodded and kept breathing as the pain hit harder then topped out and began to release its hold.

"Jess, did you call Landon again?" Cassie asked.

"Yes, still not answering. He's probably on the plane."

Emma felt an ache in her heart. This couldn't happen without him.

"You okay?" Cassie reached over and rubbed Emma's arm.

"Yeah," Emma answered, fighting to keep her emotions in check. Her forehead was damp with sweat.

"Here." Cassie handed her a napkin. "Sorry, that's all I have."

"It's great. Thanks."

"We're close. Did anyone time that last contraction?"

"It was about the same, a little over four minutes."

Something told her this labor was going to be hard and fast. Emma couldn't imagine having this baby before Landon got there.

Landon's mom was going to come that weekend and stay until the baby was born. They had everything planned!

"I'm sorry it's hurting so badly," Cassie said, changing lanes. Signs for the hospital exit began to appear.

"It does hurt, but wondering if I'd ever be able to have a baby was worse." Knowing that Margaret might have jeopardized her ability to have children had driven her crazy with worry. The day she found out she was expecting was one of the happiest of her life. "I'll go through anything I have to to bring this little guy into the world."

"Landon didn't pick up," Jess reported. "I left another message and texted him."

Cassie exited off the freeway and made a right hand turn going over a bump a little too fast.

"Ah!" Emma exclaimed, holding her stomach.

"Sorry, I didn't see that," Cassie said.

The hospital came into sight. "There it is," Jess cried.

"Okay, here's the plan. I'll pull up, and you jump out and help her inside. I'll park and bring in the bags," Cassie instructed.

"Good idea," Jess said.

Emma was consumed with worry that Landon wasn't going to make it. She was also worried she was going to have another contraction before they got there.

"We made it," Cassie exclaimed, pulling into the emergency driveway. She pulled up right in front of the doors.

Jess jumped out and raced to open Emma's door.

Emma swung one leg out and, holding her stomach, pivoted her body to get her other leg out. "Oh no," she said. "Here comes . . ."

Pain took over, and she grabbed the headrest and frame of the door. "Ahh!" she cried. There was no holding back. She felt like she was being crushed from the inside. Like her spine and hip joints were going to snap.

"Watch her!" Jess yelled at Cassie. She ran to the doors and burst inside. A moment later she returned with a man in scrubs pushing a wheelchair.

Emma's attention was quickly pulled back to the gripping pain in her lower back. She lost her breathing rhythm, and she couldn't begin to find her mental happy place. Panic added to the intensity of the contraction.

The man in scrubs positioned himself in front of her. "Ma'am, you're in the middle of a contraction?"

Emma nodded but didn't look at him.

"I'm just going to stand here with you, and when it stops we will get you inside and make you comfortable. Okay?"

She nodded again.

Sweat rolled down the side of her head, and her breathing came easier as the contraction subsided.

"How far apart are the contractions?" he asked.

"A little over four minutes," Jess answered.

"Four?" he asked in alarm. "Let's get you inside," he said to Emma.

Jess helped get her out of the car and into the chair, and then Emma was wheeled through the doors into the emergency room. Everything became a blur of activity. Before she knew it, she was changing into a hospital gown while simultaneously receiving an IV.

Another contraction came on hard. The needle on the monitor, which was attached to the band around her stomach, began dancing on a paper feed and Emma began to worry that if the pains got any worse she wouldn't be able to handle them.

"Hi, Emma, I'm your nurse, Noreen." The woman with a short, blonde bob spoke to her in calm, confident tones. "I'll be with you throughout the delivery. You did great on that contraction. It looks like it's coming down. Keep breathing. Keep it slow and calm."

Emma appreciated her coaching. Her voice helped her stay focused.

"Good, Emma. That was a big one."

"Can I get some anesthesia?"

"It's too late to give you an epidural, but we're putting something in your IV to help take the edge off the pain. By the next contraction you should notice a difference."

Emma swallowed hard. The thought of not having medication to help her the rest of the way elevated her panic level.

"You're going to be fine, Emma. You're progressing quickly."

She didn't want to progress quickly. She needed to put everything on pause so Landon could get here. If she couldn't have an epidural, she at least needed him!

And if not him, then she at least needed her friends. She looked around. Where were her friends?

"Honey, do you have someone here with you?"

"My friends brought me."

"Okay, tell me their names, and I'll go find them."

Emma told her and relaxed back on the bed while the nurse went to find Jess and Cassie. The room began to fill up as other medical personnel wheeled in carts and trays and other equipment.

Another man in scrubs she didn't recognize came in. A nurse helped him put on a gown, gloves, and a mask.

"Hello, Emma. I'm Dr. Bylund. How are you doing?"

"Where's Dr. Cannon?"

"We called him when you arrived, but he isn't sure he's going to make it in time. I'm going to cover for him until he gets here."

"Okay," Emma said. Her husband wasn't there, her friends weren't there, and now here doctor wasn't there. How did this happen? They had everything planned out.

All the emotion and intensity and excitement began to build inside until it spilled over in tears.

She didn't want to be alone. This was supposed to be shared with loved ones.

While the doctor checked her progress, she rested her head back on her pillow and shut her eyes.

The next thing she knew, the doctor was yelling out centimeters and percentages. The numbers must have been important because the activity level escalated.

She scanned the room of unfamiliar faces, hoping to see Jess or Cassie, but neither of them were with her.

Another contraction began, tightening her stomach muscles and creating pressure.

"Okay, Emma, it's almost time to push," the doctor said.

"No!" Emma said. "My husband's not here." She gritted her teeth and closed her eyes. Whatever they put in her IV had the power of a baby aspirin.

"I'm sorry, but—" the doctor began.

"Emma?" A voice from the doorway called to her.

She opened her eyes and glanced over. Immediately she burst into tears, crying out from pain and joy.

"Honey, I'm here."

Landon quickly took his place beside her and grabbed hold of her hand. "I got here as soon as I could. I took an earlier—"

"Owww!" Emma cried out, unable to hold in her pain. She gave Landon's hand a tremendous squeeze, taking him by surprise. He gasped but didn't say anything.

The contraction eased up, and she released her grip.

Nurse Noreen handed him a cool wet cloth to wipe her forehead.

"You made it," Emma said. "I was so scared you wouldn't."

"I was able to get an earlier flight." He wiped the tears from her cheeks. "I got to the airport and felt really anxious to get home. I got lucky because they were able to get me on."

"I don't think it was luck," Emma said, looking into his handsome face. She hoped Oliver looked like his daddy. The thought got her excited. In a few minutes, she would know what he looked like.

"Okay, Emma," Dr. Bylund said. "When the next contraction starts I want you to start pushing."

Emma nodded.

"You're doing great, honey," Landon said. "I'm so proud of you."

"Can I hold your hand again?" she asked.

"Um, sure."

"I didn't hurt you, did I?"

"No, not at all." He stretched his fingers and wiggled them then took her hand in his.

"I did, didn't I?"

"I'm not about to complain when you're—"

She clamped down on his hand as a contraction started with an immediate onslaught of pain.

Nurse Noreen began talking her through the motions of how to put her chin in her chest and then bear down. She groaned and pushed and prayed.

"Good," Dr. Bylund said. "A few more like that and we're going to meet a new member of your family."

He was right.

* * *

"I don't think I could be any happier," Emma said, as she looked down at the tiny little face of her son snuggled in her arms. Landon sat on the bed with her, one arm hugging her, the other arm cradling their son.

"Me either," Landon agreed. He kissed her temple, and then they rested their heads together as they gazed at their son.

"I'm pretty sure he's the cutest baby ever born."

"No question."

"He's perfect."

"Yeah, he really is."

Oliver squirmed and made some soft squeaking noises then fell back into a blissful slumber.

"Do you think he knows how much we love him?" Landon asked.

"I think so."

"How about you?" Landon said.

"What about me?"

"Do you know how much I love you?"

She turned and looked at her husband, her strength, her hero, her eternal companion. "Yes. I do. And I love you too."

They shared a brief kiss.

"I want your parents to see him," she said, cradling Oliver's head in her hand.

"Mom said she wishes she had come out sooner. She wants us to FaceTime with her later."

"We can dress him in one of those cute little outfits she sent."

"She'd like that. She's excited to finally be a grandma."

"Really? Is that why we've received a package for Oliver in the mail every day for the last week?" she joked.

Landon laughed.

"Maybe we should go visit them," she said.

Landon circled one arm around Emma and the other around their son, enveloping them all in a protective hug. "I'm really proud of you, honey. There's just one thing I can't figure out."

"Oh? What's that?"

"How a guy like me got so lucky."

Emma smiled. "Well, you have eternity to find out," she told him, resting her head on his shoulder.

ABOUT THE AUTHOR

IN THE FOURTH GRADE, MICHELE Ashman Bell was considered a daydreamer by her teacher and was told on her report card that "she has a vivid imagination and would probably do well with creative writing." Her imagination, combined with a passion for reading, has enabled Michele to live up to her teacher's prediction. She loves writing books, especially those that inspire and edify while entertaining.

Michele grew up in St. George, Utah, where she met her husband at Dixie College before they both served missions—his to Pennsylvania and hers to Frankfurt, Germany, and San Jose, California. Seven months after they returned, they were married, and they are now the proud parents of four children: Weston, Kendyl, Andrea, and Rachel; and the grandparents of Halle and Lily.

A favorite pastime of Michele's is supporting her children in all their activities, traveling both in and outside of the United States, and doing research for her books. Aside from being a busy wife and mother, Michele is a group fitness instructor and certified Zumba instructor at the Life Centre Athletic Club, 24-Hour Fitness, and Dimple Dell Recreation Center. She currently teaches the seven- and eight-year-old class in Primary.

Michele is the bestselling author of several books and Christmas booklets and has also written children's stories for the *Friend* magazine.

If you would like to be updated on Michele's newest releases or correspond with her, please send an e-mail to info@covenant-lds.com. You may also write to her in care of Covenant Communications, P.O. Box 416, American Fork, UT 84003-0416.